When the Sea Calls

by
Don Conroy

MENTOR

This Edition first published 1999 by

MENTOR PRESS
43 Furze Road,
Sandyford Industrial Estate,
Dublin 18.
Tel. (01) 295 2112/3   Fax. (01) 295 2114
e-mail: mentor1@indigo.ie

ISBN: 0 947548 99 8

A catalogue record for this book is available from the British Library

Cover Illustration: Don Conroy
Editing, Design and Layout by Mentor Press

Printed in Ireland by ColourBooks Ltd.

1 3 5 7 9 10 8 6 4 2

'And the earth was without form
. . . and darkness was upon
the face of the deep.'

GENESIS

The Author

Don Conroy is one of Ireland's most popular writers. He has written many books for children and young adults.

Well-known as an artist, wildlife expert and television personality, Don is actively involved in conservation and environmental work.

Dedicated

to

*Sorcha Neary
and
Una Hayes*

Contents

Chapter 1

AUGUST 1914
Connemara
Co. Galway

'We thought the good Lord himself had abandoned us.'
The old woman raised her washed foot up on to the
stool. 'Can you see the cursed thing, child?'

Sinéad Keogh gently ran her fingers along the Widow
O'Halloran's foot. As she located the thorn with her index
finger, the old woman jerked her leg.

'That's the place all right.' Her face contorted. 'It's hard to
believe the divil of a thorn could practically cripple a strong
woman like myself.'

'It looks infected.' Sinéad could see the green pus and the
redness that surrounded the puncture. 'I'll get some hot water
and a pin and try to remove it.'

'God bless you, child. I've been hobbling around for the past
few days on account of it.'

Sinéad went to get the pin and the hot water.

'Bring a bit of bread as well, that's good for a poultice; it will
draw out the badness. Oh, and bring some of your father's
poitín. He's the best poitín maker in the county,' she shouted
after her, 'and has the wickedest temper as well,' she mumbled
to herself. 'Where is he anyway?' the old woman enquired.

'He's gone to Galway to the Autumn Fair. He'll be back
sometime today.' Sinéad began to remove the thorn. She
pierced the skin with the needle. The old woman shrieked.
'Sorry,' said Sinéad gripping the old widow's leg with her left
hand and removing the thorn with her right hand. 'It was

deeply embedded and was a long thorn as well,' said Sinéad as she showed the widow the offending object.

'Throw it on the fire,' said the old woman. 'And may all my bad luck go with it.'

Sinéad's next task was to remove the pus, which came out easily when she pressed the skin apart. Dipping the bread into the hot water, she caked it on the wound, then tied a piece of rag around the foot.

'Rest it there for a while,' said Sinéad, 'and I'll make you something to eat.'

'Don't go to any trouble, a cut of bread would be grand. And if that's broth I'm smelling, I'll have some.'

Sinéad washed her hands and busied herself heating up the broth and cutting some bread.

'You'll make someone a good wife so you will. You must be sixteen now.'

'Nearly seventeen,' said Sinéad.

'A young woman, to be sure. Don't forget the poitín, child, and a glass. It will kill off any germs that may be lurking inside the wound.' The old woman laughed loudly.

Sinéad brought a bottle and a glass.

'Will you have a little taste yourself?' Sinéad declined; she hated the stuff. She associated it with her father's angry drunken bouts. When he was in that state he was capable of breaking up every stick of furniture in the house or setting fire to the place. He had often vented his anger on Sinéad because she reminded him of her dead mother.

'I was telling you about the famine,' said the Widow O'Halloran, as she poured herself a glass from the bottle. 'Aaahh,' she hissed. 'That's powerful stuff. Medicine! That's what it is for an old woman like me. It will help to keep out the chill, and these nights are bitter.' She filled the glass again. 'I'll nurse this one,' she grinned, 'after finishing the first so quickly.'

Sinéad put the broth on the table beside her, then sat opposite. They tucked into the warm broth and brown bread she had made earlier.

'God bless those hands of yours, child. That bread is fit for a bishop. Now I was telling you about the poor souls during the famine. I heard it from my own mother – I declare to God I don't know how she and the family survived at all.'

'Tell me all about it,' said Sinéad eagerly.

'It was all because of the cursed blight on the praties. The potato was the staple diet of the poor people – still is to be sure. Well, wasn't the land worn out and that's how the blight could attack the potatoes. The weather was shocking and before anyone knew it a terrible famine raged.' She slurped her broth and indicated she would like a drop more.

Sinéad took the empty bowl and quickly refilled it.

'Then do you know what happened?'

Sinéad was wide-eyed and anxious to know more. 'What?' she asked.

'Didn't those absentee landlords – having run up debts in England with their gambling and womanising – didn't they have the poor people evicted! Thrown out of their homes with only the clothes on their backs, into the worst weather known to God or man.'

'Could they not have sneaked back into their homes when the peelers* were gone?' Sinéad wondered.

'Dear child, how could they? Sure weren't their houses burned to the ground! They were all left homeless. I'm telling you. And now child, I'm going to tell you something that will make you sick in the pit of your stomach. While millions were

* Peelers: The police were commonly known as peelers after Sir Robert Peel, Chief Secretary of Ireland, who organised the police force.

starving and dying along the roadside, weren't the ports and harbours teeming with food and the finest cattle waiting to be exported.'

'That is terrible, horrible,' sighed Sinéad.

'Oh we don't know how lucky we are these days. I go down on my knees every day and thank the good Lord and his blessed mother.' Then she swigged some more poitín. 'Even some of our own were in on it, those rich farmers of Kildare and the likes. They didn't suffer.'

'But could the people not have tried to steal some food at the ports? Surely it wouldn't be a sin if you and your family were starving?' said Sinéad.

'God bless your innocence child. Sure wasn't the food under armed guard; no one could get near it. Besides, the people were too weak to travel, they were walking skeletons.' She sniffed and blew her nose. 'Sure didn't the famine nearly break Ireland's heart.' She emptied the glass and looked at the bottle, then looked at Sinéad.

Sinéad indicated she could have more. As the widow poured the poitín slowly, she said quietly as if seeing the whole thing in her mind's eye.

'The ones that did survive fled the country, hoping to make a new start in the far-off lands of America.' She sipped some more. 'Tragically, most of the ships became nothing more than floating coffins. But God is good and some made it to America and Canada. There they worked hard and sent money back home to their poor families.'

'Why did they have to travel so far? Couldn't they have gone to Great Britain; it was much nearer?' Sinéad retorted.

'Well, child, I can see you have a head on your shoulders. That's a very sensible reaction.' The old woman turned and bent over as if wanting to tell some deep secret. She cocked her head and looked over her shoulder, as if to check whether anyone was listening. 'That's just it, Sinéad. We're supposed to be British subjects, but the truth was they didn't want us over there and that's why the people had to make that dangerous journey across the wide Atlantic ocean to the Americas.' She pulled the shawl over her head. 'I'd better be on my way, child. God bless you for taking that thorn out. Now I know how St Paul felt.'

Sinéad looked blank.

'Didn't that poor man have a thorn in his side most of his life?' said the old woman. She stood up and rested her feet on the flagstones.

'Well, that's a gift! I can put my two feet under me without screaming with the pain of it.' She turned and looked longingly at the bottle of poitín.

'Please take it,' insisted Sinéad. 'He won't be missing it; isn't there a new batch in one of the outhouses.'

The Widow O'Halloran swiped up the bottle and corked it, then put it under her shawl. As she went out through the front door she met Billy Keogh coming in.

'Oh! Good afternoon Billy,' she said in a startled voice. He grunted a hello. 'How was Galway City?' she asked, recovering herself.

'Same as usual,' Sinéad's father grunted in reply. 'One always comes home a few pounds lighter in the pocket after a visit.'

'Sure aren't you lucky to have it. There are some that haven't so much as a thraneen* in their pockets.'

'Well, I work hard for it,' he growled. 'No one ever comes to this house to give me anything, only take.'

'Ah now that's a bit hard,' said the old widow smiling.

*Thraneen or tráithnín: a dry grass stalk.

'Hard be damned. It's true.'

'Well I must be going,' she said brightly. 'I'm off to the chapel. I'll say one for you.'

'Say it for yourself,' he mumbled.

He brushed past Sinéad and yelled, 'What did that old hag want?'

Sinéad quickly picked up the bowls and the empty glass off the table.

'Well? I asked you a question,' he said menacingly.

'Oh nothing much . . . she had a thorn in her foot that I helped to remove.'

'She probably got it in the cemetery where she goes to haunt in the nights,' he sniggered. 'Get me some food. It took me ages to get a lift for the last leg of the journey.'

'There's some boiled bacon and I made some vegetable broth and bread.'

'That will do fine.' He sat down beside the table and spilled some money from his pockets out on the table.

'A good trip to Galway, I see,' said Sinéad.

'You see too much, young lassie. Careful you don't end up like that old biddy, knowing everyone's business in every town and village around.'

Sinéad placed the food in front of him. He took off his hat, pushed the money into it, then left it on the table beside him. He tucked into the food like a ravenous dog.

Billy Keogh was tall and slim, a strong man with black wavy hair. He had just turned forty, although the permanent scowl he wore on his face made him look like a man much older. He always seemed to be at war with life and had no real friends, merely acquaintances. Sinéad was his only child and they lived in their small home by the sea. He made a living catching lobsters and doing odd jobs. He had a reputation as the finest poitín-maker in Connaught and most of his money was made that way. Regular customers came from both near and far.

'I hope that Widow O'Halloran wasn't filling your head with any wild stories about your mother.'

'No! She never talks about my mother, she was telling me all about the terrible famine.'

'The famine,' he growled. 'I've heard her, down in the shebeen*, talking about the famine. Anyone would think she was there at the time. That's one old hag that wouldn't go hungry, famine or no.'

'But her family suffered terribly,' said Sinéad.

'I don't want to talk about it. Just go and get me a bottle from the outhouse.'

'Would you not like a nice mug of tea instead, Daddy? I was going to make one for myself.'

'Don't tell me what I would like or should have. Only go and get a bottle of my own brew now!'

Sinéad hurried to the outhouse, grabbed a bottle of poitín and hurried back inside. 'Give it here,' he snapped. He pulled the cork from the bottle and was about to drink it when he paused and stared at Sinéad who was stoking the fire.

'You didn't give that old hag any of my brew?'

Sinéad placed some more turf on the fire.

'Look at me when I'm talking to you!'

'I just gave her a little to keep the chill out,' said Sinéad nervously.

He took a swig from the bottle then began to cough uncontrollably. He stood up, coughing for several minutes. Sinéad hastened over to him with a mug of water from the bucket. He pushed her away muttering, 'Leave me alone,' as he

*Shebeen or síbín: a place where alcohol was sold illegally.

took another mouthful of the poitín. 'Ah, that's better.' He wiped his mouth with the side of his hand then grabbed Sinéad by the hair. He tugged at it so hard that she felt a shooting pain in her head. 'I'm glad you didn't lie to me, missie, for if you do I'll break every bone in your body, do you understand?'

'Stop please, Daddy. It hurts.'

'Well, just you remember what I'm saying,' he cautioned, pushing her away. As he loosened his grip she fell against the table. Steadying herself, tears escaped from her eyes and she began to tremble, like a reed in the wind.

'I'm going out now to check the lobster pots.' He stopped in the doorway and stared back at her. 'You don't know how lucky you are . . . you've got a good home with plenty to eat; you never go hungry. There are people not a million miles away living in hovels – no better than rats, so you learn to have a bit of respect for your father.'

'I do,' Sinéad said.

'I could easily have hired you out from the time you were twelve, like so many of your age, who work hard from dawn to dusk on those big farms and don't see their family from the beginning of the year until Christmas. I could have made you earn your keep! Would you have liked that?'

'No Daddy!' she whimpered.

He took another drink from the bottle and glared at her. 'Don't be staring at me with those accusing eyes.'

She glanced to the floor, then with a sweep of her arms she removed the dishes from the table.

Billy Keogh walked out the door, nearly stepping on the chickens and geese that had gathered outside waiting to be fed. He kicked at them and they fluttered in different directions. The geese honked in annoyance.

Sinéad moved over to the window and as she watched him trudge down the road she began to relax. Today she'd got off lightly with a pulling of her hair. There were times when he was in a mood so fierce that she felt the leather strap of his belt across her back. On one occasion he had thrown a metal mug at her which cut her just below the eye.

She wondered were all men like this at home, yet she knew so many men in the village who were friendly and kind to her. At times like this she wished she had her mother around. What she knew of her mother was just snippets she had heard from the Widow O'Halloran and some of the other women of the village. All they ever said was how beautiful Sylvia was and how she was wasted on the likes of Billy Keogh.

Sinéad went into her bedroom and took down from the wall the only picture she had of her mother. She was so beautiful. It was taken in Dublin. In the photograph Sylvia Keogh had her arms around her husband. She looked so demure and graceful, with a neck like a swan. Her black hair was pulled back, framing her face, and gathered at the back. Billy looked very handsome, and a little funny with a thin moustache. He seemed very still and looked uncomfortable in his pose.

Sinéad longed to know more about her mother. She imagined her being a gay and happy woman, always singing and dancing. The young girl tried to put the few pieces of information that she had heard together like a jigsaw puzzle, but there were too many pieces missing. Her father never spoke of his wife except to say she had left him with the burden of bringing up a child on his own. The Widow O'Halloran spoke of her as if she were some kind of saint 'not belonging to this world at all'. Sinéad wanted so much to find out more about the beautiful woman in the faded photograph, but asking

people was like pulling teeth, they were all so reluctant to tell her anything.

Was there some dark secret that kept people from talking? It was as if there was a conspiracy of silence. Sinéad had received some information through her friend Ciara Mack, who had pumped her own father and mother for news. It was helpful but very sketchy and Sinéad was determined to find out more.

Sinéad went and cleared up the kitchen, then she fed the hens and the geese. Knowing her father would head down to Johnny Mack's after he had checked the lobster pots, Sinéad decided to walk up to the cliffs. A light breeze blew in from the sea as she made her way across the bog towards the cliffs. Ahead, a hare bolted from its cover and padded off only to stop a few yards away. A hooded crow lifted from a dead tree stump and moved silently over the bog. As Sinéad made her way along the cliffs she looked back to see if she could get a glimpse of her home. She was barely able to make out the thatched roof, but she could see the blue smoke rising from the chimney.

Sinéad pulled her shawl tightly around her as she eased herself onto a limestone boulder and stared pensively out to sea. These barren cliffs had become her oasis. Any chance she got she would come up here. Sun, rain or fog she didn't care. There was a freedom in these wild places that gave her a sense of tranquility. On an evening like this with the afterglow of a sunset, Sinéad could marvel and enjoy the sheer beauty of the place.

She would also come here to ease the pain during her long periods of loneliness. She would imagine the giant rocks that rose out of the bog to be a secret castle that closed in on itself during the day, but at night by the light of a full moon opened out into a splendid castle that she alone knew how to enter.

As the light began to fade Sinéad noticed movement in the dark waters. A dolphin broke the surface. Several others soon appeared. They frolicked about for a short time, then began to porpoise away out to sea. Sinéad looked at them excitedly – it was her first time to see dolphins. She counted five. Were they always out there, she wondered. If they were, she had never seen them before.

Then she remembered something the Widow O'Halloran had said to her when she was twelve or thirteen, that the big fish were messengers from another world. The old woman was about to say more when Father Darcy had come up the road. Despite Sinéad's coaxing, the widow never brought up the subject again. However, she had learned from the widow that her mother loved swimming. Sinéad knew she had that in common with her mother: she loved the sea in its many moods. There was such a sense of freedom when she swam in the crystal clear waters.

Chapter 2

Johnny Mack's shebeen was packed to capacity. It was as if the entire village had turned up to listen to the wandering scholar, Hugh Lynskey.

Sinéad and the other village girls were always asked to help out at special events, for it was expected of Johnny Mack to provide meals and drinks on these occasions. A big, ruddy-faced man, Johnny Mack had a broad smile and a warm handshake. He would give the girls a few pennies for their help and let them bring home any leftover food.

Some folk travelled great distances to hear the scholar. He would always have wonderful stories to relate and perhaps teach them something about their own history.

Hugh Lynskey stood beside the hearth. He was a tall, thin man with a fine, red beard. He wore a wide-brimmed hat and had a rope tied around his waist. In his right hand he held a hazel stick, a glass of porter in his left. It was said he came originally from Galway City but no one was sure. He claimed to have walked the length and breadth of Ireland, that he could read and write in several languages, and that the books he had read could fill the library of Trinity College.

'*Ciúnas*!' shouted Johnny Mack from behind the counter. 'And give a good Connemara welcome to Hugh Lynskey: an honourable man, a storyteller and scholar all rolled into one.'

'Good on yeh, Johnny Mack!' yelled an old man sitting in the corner.

'You're welcome and God bless you,' said the Widow O'Halloran to the visitor.

Hugh Lynskey took another sip from the glass of porter then cleared his throat. 'A man who walks the road sees many a strange thing . . .' He paused for effect, to let the comment sink in with the listeners.

'Too true!' said Dingy O'Rourke as he emptied his glass of stout.

'Quiet,' yelled another. 'Let the man talk.'

Hugh Lynskey continued: '. . . and the strangest thing I've seen was on my way in to Ballinasloe.'

'What was it?' shouted a young lad. 'The Queen of Sheba?' he laughed.

'Kevin Darcy, keep quiet!' His mother scolded him from the other side of the room.

Hugh Lynskey stared hard at the young man then continued. 'Oh it must be a year to this day. It was dark and cold like tonight. The moon hung in all her glory in the sky and you could see the broad ring around it. Well, here I was heading to the town, minding my own business, when didn't a vixen give out a scream the likes of which you have never heard. It was like the wail of the banshee. Well, I crossed myself three times I got such a start.

'Now, you may think that I'd never heard a fox calling to her mate before, but this was no ordinary call. It was like a warning cry telling me to beware of something. Sure, in a moment I recovered myself . . . and seeing the warm light of the village my courage returned to me. Then I was stopped in my tracks. My feet felt stuck to the ground, for to the right of me was the cemetery, and from behind one of the tombstones stood a tall man of my own height and build. He beckoned me with his hand. Sure I couldn't move, wasn't I rooted with fear! He stood there in the silvery light just waving at me to come over.

24

Well, before I knew it I was alongside him. Oh, he was a handsome man with a fine black suit the likes you'd see on a gentleman in Dublin, London or Paris. Yet there was something about his stare that made me uneasy. I asked him had he lost a loved one and was that the reason he stood so, all alone in a cemetery. He gave me the strangest of smiles, then invited me to join him for a drink in a nearby tavern. Well, I can tell you all here . . . I was in a dilemma, for he seemed friendly enough but it was most peculiar that someone would be standing all alone in a cemetery at that hour.'

'Was it the divil himself?' asked Mrs Darcy.

'You hit the nail on the head,' he pointed his finger at her.

Most of the older people crossed themselves.

Billy Keogh mumbled under his breath. 'Wait for it,' he said to Paddy Gilmore who was sitting alongside him. 'He'll have tricked the devil into giving him something, then he'll tell us how he outsmarted Old Nick.'

'What happened then?' asked another, as Sinéad replaced the scholar's empty glass with a full one.

Hugh Lynskey stared at Sinéad in a strange way. 'Thank you, young lady,' he said, accepting the drink.

'Over here,' shouted her father, waving his empty glass.

Sinéad hurried behind the counter to get her father a glass of porter.

'Well, didn't we go on into the town and stop at the nearest tavern,' Lynskey continued. 'I don't mind telling you I was glad to get out of the cold winds. There we sat with the finest of cognac in front of us. I was glad he was paying, for I didn't have two thraneens of my own to rub together. "You're a scholar," he said to me. Well, I wondered how he knew that for he couldn't tell it by my attire. "I am," I said proudly. Then he bade me ask him any question about the history of any country in the world. I knew he too must be a learned man by his appearance and dress sense, and of course his cultured accent.'

'Was it an English accent?' Billy Keogh yelled up. This caused a laugh among some of the listeners.

'Did he look like Oliver Cromwell?' shouted Dingy O'Rourke. This brought more laughter.

'Well, I'm not going to continue if I'm going to get any more interruptions. I'll go to an establishment that will appreciate my words of wisdom.'

Johnny Mack moved quickly out from behind the counter and over to Hugh Lynskey. 'Now hold on, Mr Lynskey. They're a bit skittish, those people who have just returned from Galway City.' He glared at Billy Keogh and Dingy O'Rourke. 'I promise there will be no more interruptions from any that want to stay here to listen to your fine words and grand stories.'

Hugh Lynskey seemed satisfied by Johnny Mack's assurance. He handed Johnny Mack his empty glass, indicating he needed another refill. 'Well, didn't I put him to the test! I asked him as many a difficult question as I could think of, including ones I didn't know the answer to myself,' he grinned.

'I asked him when the great city of Rome was founded. "753 BC," he answered. "When was the siege of Troy?" "1180 BC." "When was Alexander the Great born?" "356 BC; he died in 323 BC." "Where did he die?" I asked. "In Babylon," he replied.

'I asked him who was Augustus? "He was the first Roman Emperor, between 63 BC and 14 AD; adopted son of his great uncle Julius Caesar."

'"When did George Washington become president of America?" "He took office in 1789, he was a federalist," the stranger answered, smiling.

'"When did Wellington beat Napoleon?" "Well, this battle finally ended on the 18 June 1815, south of Brussels at Waterloo, Wellington with 68,000 troops and Napoleon with 72,000. Of course, towards the end of the battle Wellington got some help from the Russians."

'Bedad, he was a walking encyclopaedia. For those who don't know what that is, it's a fine book containing all the important information about the world.'

'Did you ask him about dear old Ireland?' the Widow O'Halloran shouted up at him.

'I did, fine woman, I did. He told me that the great book, *The Book of Kells*, was illuminated in the eighth century.'

'That's a grand word,' said the Widow O'Halloran. 'Illuminated!'

'He told me that Brian Boru became High King of Ireland in 1002 AD. He told me that it was an English pope who gave Ireland to Henry II in a Papal Bull.'

'I wouldn't believe that,' shouted Peadar Walsh. 'That's a lie!' he flared. 'Don't let Father Darcy hear you saying that.'

'Ah, don't be getting so worked up,' said Dingy O'Rourke. 'Sure wasn't the good Saint Patrick English, or was he Welsh?'

'St Patrick was an Irishman through and through!' Peadar Walsh banged his fist on the table.

'Will you two keep quiet,' said the Widow O'Halloran, 'and let the man finish his story?' Hugh Lynskey cleared his throat.

'Well, after all the fine conversation,' he continued, 'didn't he turn to me and, in a deadly serious voice, didn't he offer me all the wisdom of the ages and a large purseful of golden sovereigns?' He drank down the third glass of porter.

'It was the divil, I knew it,' shouted a woman.

'Aye,' agreed another.

'What did he want? And what did you do?' Johnny Mack asked anxiously.

'I think you all know what the devil wants,' said Hugh Lynskey in sinister tones. 'He was after my immortal soul. Didn't he want to play on my weakness and me a man with a hunger for knowledge. And a poor man as well. Well, I don't mind telling you I was sorely tempted, looking at that bright gold gleaming up at me from the table. Well, I looked him in the eye and, drawing on all the strength I could muster, I told him that all the knowledge I had was hard earned and that's the way I prefer it. As for my soul, didn't the good Lord himself go to a cross for the likes of me.'

'Well said!' shouted up an old woman.

'That took some courage,' said another.

'What did he do then?' asked a third.

'He smiled and put away the purse of golden coins and said: never mind, there are others willing to trade. He rose to his feet and bade me goodnight. Excuse me, said I stretching my courage. How can the likes of you bear the torments of hell?'

'Well, that was a daring question to ask Old Nick,' shouted the Widow O'Halloran.

'Do you know what he said?'

There was a deathly silence as Hugh Lynskey looked around at the crowd.

'"What makes it bearable is that I still carry the voice of God in my head." He said this in a sort of melancholy tone. Then he turned to leave. None of the other customers took a blind bit of notice of him for he just looked like an ordinary well-to-do gent. But didn't I notice that he cast no shadow. Well, all of a sudden he stopped in his tracks and looked back at me, and he said something to me that nearly froze me to the spot.'

Again he emptied his glass of porter and rubbed his stomach to indicate he was hungry.

Johnny Mack, who was watching the old scholar like a hawk, called to the girls to pass around the plates of food and he immediately poured another glass of porter for him.

'Don't leave us in suspense,' shouted Dingy O'Rourke. 'Tell us what he said.'

Hugh Lynskey played the pause like a great actor, then said with a deep strong voice: '"This century belongs to me." He gave a deadly grin then left the tavern.'

There was a shocked silence.

Johnny Mack hurried over to the scholar and patted him on the back. 'Good on yeh, Hugh Lynskey, resisting the temptation of Old Nick himself . . .' Then he elbowed the old scholar, ' . . . and getting him to buy you a drink.'

The crowd laughed and cheered.

'Time for some music,' Johnny Mack commanded.

The musicians took up their instruments and began to tune them. Sinéad nervously handed a plate of food to the scholar. He took it and stared hard at Sinéad.

'Where are you from, young lady?' he asked.

'A few miles west of the village,' she replied.

He placed the forefinger of his right hand under her chin and raised her face. Their eyes locked for a moment. Then Sinéad turned away. 'You're different,' he said softly. 'I can always tell. Your eyes hold secrets.' His tone was almost menacing.

The Widow O'Halloran watched the old scholar with Sinéad. She could see the young girl becoming distressed so she rose to her feet and grabbed Sinéad by the arm.

'Listen Sinéad, would you ever get me some of that food like a good child. The sight of it is putting the longing on me,' and with that she ushered her away.

The music began and some started to dance. The sounds of merrymaking filled the shebeen. As the music and dancing was in full swing, a stranger slowly entered by the side door. Silence descended. All eyes stared at the tall handsome stranger.

He looked at the large gathering and said quietly. 'Good evening.'

All eyes followed as he made his way towards the counter. Johnny Mack stood motionless with his mouth slightly parted, a bottle in one hand and a half-filled glass in the other.

The stranger smiled and said, 'I wonder would you have a room for a night or two?'

Chapter 3

Johnny Mack laughed uproariously. 'By God we thought you were Old Nick himself when you arrived like that yesterday in the dead of night.'

Richard Anderson smiled warmly.

'Well, did you sleep at all with the racket last night?'

'I slept like a log, thank you.'

Johnny Mack's daughter, Ciara, arrived over with a large breakfast of bacon, sausages and eggs and placed it in front of him. She smiled at Richard with her eyes then hurried away.

'I put your bike in the shed,' said Johnny Mack. 'I see you got yourself a puncture. Where did that happen?

'About eight miles out the road. I was coming from Galway,' said Richard.

'That's a fair cycle from Galway to here. I never got used to the bike myself, I prefer the horse and cart. I think the bicycle is a bit of a circus act, with two little wheels underneath you.'

Richard Anderson grinned as he tucked into the breakfast.

'Oh God, you haven't got your tea yet. Ciara! Ciara!' She popped her head around the door. 'For the love of God girl will you get the poor man a mug of tea and some bread!'

'The water's just coming to the boil, Daddy. I'll bring it out in a minute.'

Johnny Mack laughed. 'We were all a bit late getting to bed last night. You missed a grand talk by one of our finest wandering scholars, a man called Hugh Lynskey.'

Ciara hurried out with the bread and tea.

'Thank you.' He extended his hand to her. 'I'm Richard Anderson.' Ciara wiped her hand in her apron then shook his.

Johnny Mack sat down beside the stranger. 'That's no Galway accent or any born on this island.'

'I'm a Londoner,' said Richard.

'London,' said Johnny Mack. 'Oh I hear it's a fine city. With Big Ben, the Houses of Parliament and all. Not that I've ever been there, sure I've hardly been around Ireland. Too busy running this place . . . always something to be done,' he sighed. 'What do you do yourself? If it's not too personal a question.'

'Well, I have a few strings to my bow, so to speak. I write, illustrate books and try my hand at poetry.'

'Well, that's fine work indeed, I can see it in your hands that you're not used to the outdoor work.'

'Oh I've done my share of outdoor work when I was in Africa.'

'You've been to Africa?' said Johnny Mack in awe.

'Oh, I've been to lots of places. I was with the 44th Battery, Royal Artillery during the Boer War – or the South Africa war – which began in 1899. I arrived in 1901 and thankfully the war ended in 1902. I was a war artist. I was asked to make creative sketches of people maiming and killing each other for the newspapers and magazines and get paid for it. My work appeared mainly in the *London Weekly* and *Sphere*, with several pages of my sketches depicting the Battle of Karreebosch Poort.'

Johnny Mack could see the smile vanish from the young man's face as he spoke about it. Richard finished his tea, looked out the window as if in a trance then said in bitter tones: 'They're starting again, oiling the war machine.'

Ciara came out from the back room and took the empty plate and mug. 'Would you like some more tea?'

'No thanks,' he said brightly.

'Would you have any of your sketches so I could have a glimpse of them?' asked Johnny Mack.

Richard Anderson went to his room and returned with a leather satchel. He took out a sketchbook and handed it to Johnny Mack.

Ciara looked over her father's shoulder. There were colour sketches of people, cottages, animals, trees, flowers and birds. Johnny Mack's big hands gently leafed through the sketchbook.

'Well, God bless your hands,' he remarked. 'I've never seen the likes of it.' As they looked at a robin perched on a post, Ciara remarked that it looked like it could fly off the page.

'Well thank you,' said Richard. 'I couldn't ask for a better compliment than that.'

'The robin is my favourite,' said Ciara.

Richard took the sketchpad and tore the page from it. 'There you are, young lady, a present.'

'Well, I'll be . . .' declared Johnny Mack. 'You look after that now, child, and make sure no greasy fingers touch that fine picture.'

'That's very kind of you,' said Ciara, ignoring her father's remark.

'Well, your ears must be red,' said the Widow O'Halloran to Richard as she passed through the doorway into the shebeen. Looking at the others she said warmly, 'The blessings of God on you all.' Johnny Mack introduced the stranger to the widow. 'You nearly gave us all a heart attack last night with your arrival at such a late hour. An Englishman is it?' said the widow, folding her arms and eyeing him up and down. 'I thought most of you Englishmen never went further than Dublin or Belfast. Are you a soldier or a policeman or what?'

'I was,' he replied, 'a soldier . . .' clarifying the situation. 'Now I'm a jack of all trades.'

Johnny Mack, becoming familiar, took the sketchbook from him and passed it over to the widow. 'Feast your eyes on that.'

The Widow O'Halloran took the pad; she was a little taken aback by the request. Then she opened a page at random and saw several drawings of hens.

'Well, I declare to God aren't they just marvellous. Did you do them?'

'He did,' said Johnny Mack answering for Richard.

'What's the likes of a fine gentleman like you doing in these parts?' the Widow O'Halloran asked, dying with curiosity.

'Well, I just wanted to get out of London for a while and the west of Ireland always appealed to me. I plan to stay for a few months, maybe longer.' Johnny Mack looked at the Widow O'Halloran. 'I'd like to buy or rent a place near the village. Is that possible?' he added.

'Well, there's not many cottages around here that aren't occupied by big families,' said Johnny Mack.

'What about the McMahons' dwelling?' said the widow. 'You'd need to talk to Dermot McGrath; he'd know all about that place.'

'It's a ruin of a place,' said Johnny Mack.

'It's near the shore. There's a twisted ash tree bent by the winds,' said the widow. 'It practically points to the place,' she grinned.

'You'll hardly see the cottage,' said Johnny Mack, chuckling to himself. 'But it's there. Just look over the nettles.'

This brought loud laughter.

'Ah, he's only teasing,' said the widow linking the stranger by the arm. 'Come with me and I'll introduce you to Dermot

McGrath.' She began to usher him out of the shebeen. Then she stopped. 'I'll forget my head if I'm not careful,' she quipped, turning to Johnny Mack. 'Any chance of some tea and sugar? I can't function in the morning without a cup of tea inside me.' Johnny Mack produced a tin of tea leaves and some sugar. 'The blessings of God on you,' she said. Then winking she continued, 'Put it on the slate like a good man, and I'll be in to you next week with the money.'

'Allow me,' said Richard, offering to pay for the tea and sugar.

Johnny Mack took the ten-shilling note and hurried into the back for change.

'Well may God reward you for your kindness,' said the widow. 'We'll find McGrath and you'll come back to my cottage. I'll make you a nice cup of tea and you'll tell me all about yourself and that fine city of London. I'll see you tonight, Johnny Mack and you too, Ciara dear. But for now I'll escort this handsome gent down the road,' she grinned broadly.

Chapter 4

'We're in luck,' said the Widow O'Halloran. 'There's McGrath coming down the road now.'

They watched the silhouetted form of a man and a donkey heading towards them.

'*Dia daoibh*,' said the man as he approached.

'Dermot McGrath, the very man,' said the widow.

Richard Anderson looked at the hollow-cheeked man as he stood with his donkey, and his dog sitting on its back.

'That wind would skin you across the bog,' said Dermot McGrath jerking his shoulders.

'Fine dry turf there,' said the widow, as she looked at the two panniers of turf, one on either side of the donkey. 'Let me introduce you to Mr Anderson, come all the way from London.'

'Pleased to meet you,' said Dermot McGrath extending his big strong hand. Richard shook it warmly. 'Well, you've a fine strong handshake,' said Dermot McGrath. 'I like that. You can tell a lot about someone by his handshake.'

Richard smiled and then patted the dog on the head.

'That's Smokey,' said his owner. 'He's great company, like Nelly here.' McGrath scratched the donkey below the chin.

'We have a proposition to put to you,' said the widow. 'But we'll not stand out here discussing it. Come over to my place, it's not a stone's throw away, and I'll make you some tea and give you a slice of the brack young Sinéad Keogh made for me.'

A curlew called. Richard Anderson looked around, then spotted it flying low towards the seashore. A small brown bird flew from a dry stone wall across the road to the far wall.

'A meadow pipit,' remarked Richard.

'Well, I never knew its name before,' said Dermot McGrath as they ambled down the road. 'They're all just birdeens to me.'

'Sure isn't it grand to see them,' said the widow. 'The little innocents!'

'Oh, I could tell you where they nest and the type of call they make and how many young they'd have,' said McGrath, 'but I never knew the names.'

'Well it's just that I'm interested in ornithology.'

The widow looked blankly.

'I like bird-watching,' Richard added.

'Well, isn't that a grand and innocent pastime,' said the widow. They arrived at her cottage, a fine cottage with a recently thatched roof. In an adjoining field, a Connemara pony looked over the wall. Richard walked over to it and stroked its head.

'That's not mine,' said the widow. 'But there are times I think it is, for it's always coming around the back of the house looking for food. It loves bread with a sprinkle of sugar on it. Sometimes at night it will sleep in my field and I declare to God I'm sure I end up dreaming the horse's dreams.'

They all laughed loudly.

'Isn't that true?' she asked the horse jokingly scratching it along its neck. 'It belongs to Tom Ward's youngest daughter, Cathleen.'

Richard pulled out a small notebook and pencil and did a quick sketch of the head of the horse. The widow smiled approvingly to Dermot.

'Tom Ward is from Galway, has a shop and all in the city. He told me these horses can be traced back to the wild horses of the ice age and that the Celts brought them to these shores. Then in the last century didn't they cross them with Arab steeds.'

'Well, you're a mine of information,' declared Dermot McGrath.

The widow elbowed him. 'Go on out of that with your teasing. I'm only repeating what Tom Ward told me.'

'That's very interesting indeed,' said Richard.

'Come inside,' said the widow. 'And we'll get down to the business of getting you a roof over your head. Fresh water from the spring,' she added, lifting up a tin jug. She went about making the tea, then she sliced up the brack. They sat around the table eating and chatting.

The widow had given the man's donkey some beet, and the dog a rabbit carcass that she had boiled up for broth.

'That's a lovely bit of brack,' said Dermot McGrath as he helped himself to another slice of it.

'That's young Sinéad Keogh's. She's is a grand young woman,' said the widow. 'And so kind. Her father on the other hand is a cold article,' she grumbled. 'I don't think anyone really knows him; he's a man at war with the world and himself.'

'Terrible shame about her mother,' added Dermot. 'How long is it now since her death? Fifteen years?'

'No, it's nearly seventeen,' said the widow. 'Listen, poor Mr Anderson didn't come to listen to us taking about village life.'

'Please call me Richard,' he offered.

'Well, Richard here is a fine artist and has come to stay for a time in these parts. He's staying up with Johnny Mack at present but wants a place of his own.'

Dermot McGrath took off his cap and scratched his wisps of grey hair. He was listening intently.

'Now here's where you come in,' she touched his arm. 'I suggested he might talk to you about the McMahons' dwelling. I know it's only an old ruin of a thing, but it's the only place I can think of. It's not much use to you, and the McMahons are long gone. The place is rightfully yours since you were related to them.'

'Sure you'd be no better than a fox there, for there's no roof or nothing,' exclaimed Dermot.

'Has he got the place if he gives you the money for it?' Then she added, 'And I know a decent Christian man like you won't charge him the earth for it.'

'Well then, I'd be delighted to let you have it for a fair price.' He spat on his hand. 'Shake on it.'

Richard shook Dermot's hand.

'Well, that's settled.' The widow beamed, winking at Richard.

After they worked out the price Dermot offered to roof the house. He would put a straw roof on it instead of rushes.

'Fine golden mellow straw like this place, and I'll put a thick fringe of stones to hang along the eaves.'

'You'll need that,' said the widow, 'with the winter winds we get around here.'

'Well, I'm very grateful,' said Richard. 'Last night I was wondering what I would do as I pushed my bike with its punctured tyre. Today I'm organised with a cottage by the sea.'

'Hold your horses,' said the widow. 'It'll be several weeks before you can move into McMahons' cottage – in the meantime you're welcome to move in here with me. There's a grand, clean bedroom over there with a settle bed. I'd welcome the company. It would be free of charge. Maybe you might do the odd job around the place for me. Nothing too demanding with your fine soft hands,' she laughed.

'Well, it's very kind of you but—'

'I won't take any buts,' retorted the widow. 'As long as Father Darcy doesn't shame me from the pulpit about a handsome stranger living under my roof,' she laughed even louder.

'Well, I better be off,' said Dermot, calling his dog.

'Sure go with him,' the widow urged Richard, 'and he can show you the old cottage. Collect your things from Johnny Mack's and I'll cook you a nice supper on your return.'

'Thank you both for your kindness,' said Richard.

Chapter 5

Sinéad had a fitful sleep. Perhaps she had become overtired and that was the reason she kept waking during the night. She was in a cold sweat when she awoke. It had been a wonderful night in Johnny Mack's place. The wandering scholar was very interesting even if he did put the heart across his listeners telling them of his encounter with the devil. But the evening had been marred a bit by her father's behaviour, getting so drunk that she practically had to carry him to the jaunting car along with Dingy O'Rourke and Peadar Walsh.

She ended up driving them home because they were all too drunk to steer the horse. Sinéad, who had never driven one of these traps before, was completely stressed out not knowing whether she was giving the horse too much rein or too little. She certainly didn't like the idea of hitting the horse with a hazel stick; it used to upset her so much watching her father lash the poor horse when he was driving.

It was bad enough steering the jaunting car with three drunken men on board but going down the lonely roads half expecting the devil or a banshee to appear out of nowhere scared the life out of her. At one point a hare ran across the road and nearly made the horse rear.

It had taken her all her strength to drag Dingy O'Rourke from the jaunting car and point him in the direction of his farm. Peadar Walsh was almost impossible to shift with his big frame; Sinéad and himself ended up falling from the car as she tried to support him. Luckily there was no injury to either of them. His cottage was near the roadside so it was a little easier to deposit him at his doorstep.

Her father decided to get sick along a rough patch of road all over the back of the jaunting car. By the time she got him home and put him to bed she was a trembling wreck. She had to wash out the inside of the car and put the horse in the field before she finally got to bed.

Sinéad got out of bed, washed her face and checked in on her father who was snoring soundly. He was still in his clothes. Sinéad had removed his boots. Out towards the beach she went. She was feeling very groggy and the smoke in the shebeen last night had made her eyes sting. When she arrived at the seashore a flock of oystercatchers took to the air. She watched them fly low over the water.

Sinéad tested the water with her foot. It was cold. The sunlight on the water made it look so inviting. She looked around to see if anyone was about. The place was deserted. She threw off her clothes and ran into the glistening waves. The chilly water made her gasp. Then she dived below the waves and swam several strokes before bobbing up. She shrieked from the cold and her body shivered uncontrollably. She pushed her hair from her eyes and looked back to the shore.

Sinéad loved the water; none of the villagers ever entered it except to get into the boats. Sinéad could not understand it. The sea brought her such a sense of joy and freedom. She began to do the breaststroke and swam out beyond the rocks. She warmed up as she swam about. In the distance a grey seal bobbed its head above the water to take a breath, then slipped below the surface.

Sinéad weaved in and out through the waves. Many of the local people were fearful of the water but not her. It was as if she belonged here. She felt alive in this cold beauty, this great solitude they call the sea. Yet she knew it could hold great danger especially during a winter storm when it rose like a sleeping giant and raged towards the shore, its waves climbing the height of the cliffs and tearing at them. She had seen where the cliffs had fallen away from the sea's assault. But today it was as calm as a lake.

Sinéad swam with confident strokes parallel to the dark cliffs. She could see the green land push out to the cliff tops. Yellow gorse and patches of purple heather dotted the landscape.

It was wonderful to be able to look at the cliffs from the water. She could pick out her favourite rock where she liked to sit and look out at the sea. Sinéad suddenly became aware that she was being watched. Turning quickly she saw them, and the sight made her tremble. She had seen them for the first time yesterday from the cliffs and now they were only an arm's stretch away.

They circled her slowly. She felt a mixture of terror and excitement. The pod of dolphins moved effortlessly through the water. It was their domain, she was the alien, the land creature. They slowed and pulled themselves into an upright position. Sinéad moved her body in a clockwise motion taking in each one. They stared back with their liquid black eyes, eyes that seemed to bore right into her being, not in a threatening way, more like a camera that wished to capture an image.

Then as quickly as they appeared they left, dropping silently below the surface. It all seemed to happen so fast, Sinéad felt like one who had been awoken from a dream. There was no ripple in the water, no indication that they were ever there. But they had been, and she had seen them, however briefly. How different from when she watched them from the cliffs; they were moving in a leisurely way then, gently breaking the mirror surface. This time it was as if they were checking her out, as if

they had a wish to make contact with her. Fishermen had said they were very curious creatures and were known to have instigated numerous close encounters.

Now that they were gone and the realisation had sunk in, Sinéad felt exhilarated. She splashed the water and called joyfully to the sky. She swam, trying to mimic their movements through the water. After a time she headed for shore and got dressed.

There was a strong breeze blowing from the land as she worked her way up to the bog. A stonechat flew from a gorse bush then perched a little further along on the drystone wall. A wren skulked below it and they darted for cover among the brambles. Sinéad ran towards the cottage. She could feel the wind moving through her long hair, lifting it and drying it as she ran.

As she entered the cottage she could hear her father snoring away on his bed. She sneaked over and looked in on him. He was still out for the count. She grabbed something to eat, fed the geese and the chickens then decided to head down to visit the Widow O'Halloran.

The widow looked out the window and saw Sinéad hurrying down the road. She went out to greet her.

'How are you, child?' asked the widow warmly.

'Fine, thank the good Lord,' said Sinéad.

'Come in and have a nice cup of tea, Sinéad dear. Is there anything up?' she wondered.

'No,' said Sinéad.

'Well you ran down that boreen like someone scalded.'

Sinéad smiled. 'Did you enjoy yourself last evening?' she enquired.

'Ah, it was grand. Old Lynskey nearly put the heart across me with his stories. Still, where would we be without a good tale to tell, sure talking keeps one sane,' she added.

Sinéad asked about her foot. She could see the old woman moving about with ease.

'Oh, since you took out that wretched thorn I'm like a new woman.' She stoked up the fire, put more turf on it, and put some water into a black pot.

'Wasn't it very strange when that man came a-calling to the shebeen so late,' said Sinéad. The widow smiled.

'Later I had to drive my father home along with Dingy O'Rourke and Peadar Walsh. I was terrified I can tell you,' she continued. 'I was expecting something evil to pop out from behind a furze bush or from under the heather.'

'Some of those roads are shocking lonely at night-time,' the widow offered.

'Do you think the stranger might have been one of those demons that walk the earth or Satan himself?'

'Why don't you ask him?' smiled the widow.

Sinéad looked blankly at the old woman. Just then there was a gentle knock on the half door.

'Come on in, Mr Anderson.' He entered. Sinéad turned nervously and stared at him wide-eyed.

'Take that frightened rabbit look off,' said the widow pushing her gently. 'This is my new lodger come to stay with me for a time.'

Richard Anderson extended his hand to Sinéad. She looked at it then stared up at him.

'Take it, child, he's not going to bite you.'

He took her hand and shook it warmly. 'Richard Anderson.' Sinéad opened her mouth but no words came out.

'This is Sinéad Keogh. The nicest kindest young woman you're ever likely to meet.' Sinéad could feel herself blushing.

The widow ordered her lodger to sit down and have a cup of tea. 'I wasn't expecting you back so soon.'

'I thought I'd fix my puncture here and leave my bike in the outhouse.' The widow brought some tea and scones to the table.

'I hope they're all right. I'm not as good a cook as young Sinéad here, but I got a fine bag of flour from the parish priest, Father Darcy, for doing a bit of sewing for him. He wanted two letters sewn on a white altar cloth, alpha and omega, and a golden cross. It looked grand if I say so myself.'

'Alpha and omega, the beginning and the end,' said Richard.

'That's right,' said the widow. 'Mr Anderson is a very learned man.' She laid her hand on his shoulder. 'He writes articles and paints gorgeous pictures. You'll have to show them to Sinéad sometime.'

'I would be delighted,' he smiled.

Sinéad clutched her mug nervously.

The widow laughed as she poured out the tea.

'Didn't half the village think you were the devil himself, even Sinéad was saying it before you arrived in.' Sinéad looked extremely embarrassed. 'Wait a minute – I've some rhubarb jam you can have with those scones.' Sinéad looked down at her mug awkwardly.

'It's okay,' he smiled. 'I'm not the devil.'

The widow returned and sat with them placing the jar of jam down on the table.

'Of course you're not,' she grinned. 'For didn't I put a drop of holy water in your tea earlier to test you.'

Richard nearly gagged on his tea.

'Ha, ha.' The widow clapped him on the back and chuckled. Sinéad broke out into a laugh. Richard recovered and wiped his mouth. The widow buttered the scones and put a thick layer of jam on them.

'Eat up,' she commanded the two of them. 'Are you not afraid wandering the roads after dark?' she asked after a while.

'What's to fear in these parts?' said Richard. 'There are no dangerous wild animals or poisonous snakes to fear.'

'Would you not be afraid of a ghost or a devil crossing your path on a dark, lonely road?'

'No,' he said. 'I don't believe in the devil, or ghosts, or the boogie man.'

'You don't believe in the devil?' asked Sinéad in amazement.

'No,' he said gently. 'They're all just a job lot of fairy tales designed to control us through fear.'

'Sure where does evil come from if it's not the devil,' insisted the widow.

'I believe in evil,' he said strongly. 'But I believe it comes from man himself. It's man who chooses the way of good or evil, we can't go blaming it on some fantastic character.'

'Well, I don't know where you get those notions from,' said the widow, 'but I'm sure Father Darcy could put you straight on a few things.'

Richard smiled. 'I'm rightly reprimanded,' he retorted.

'Why would you think like that?' asked Sinéad, becoming very curious.

'Well, it's a long story but the main reason is that I have travelled a great deal in this world and have been in war situations, and what I've learned is this: if we keep blaming outside forces for our evils then we will never get to the root of the problem.'

'What you say makes a power of sense,' said the widow, pouring him out another cup of tea, 'but I'm too long in the tooth to be learning new foreign ideas like yours.'

'What do you think, Sinéad?' he asked.

'I don't really know. I believe people may be flawed but I don't think they are bad.'

'See, Mr Anderson, Sinéad may not have travelled like you but she has a head on her shoulders.'

'Call me Richard,' he insisted. 'I come from a family that would stifle you with formality. I agree with you,' he smiled warmly looking at Sinéad.

She smiled back, then turning to the widow she said brightly, 'Something extraordinary happened to me earlier.'

'And what is that, child?' the widow enquired.

'Well I was swimming earlier —'

'I declare to God, child, you'll get your death doing that,' the widow grumbled.

'No,' said Sinéad. 'It was wonderful. Anyway . . . five big grey dolphins came over to me.' The widow's face paled. Sinéad continued. 'I swear if they could talk they would have spoken to me.'

The widow grabbed Sinéad firmly by the arm.

'Keep away from those big fish,' she pleaded.

'But they didn't do me any harm, they just seemed curious.'

'Listen to me child, I'm asking you to keep well away from them.'

'Oh, they're quite harmless,' offered Richard. 'To people anyway. They are not really fish, they are mammals like us,' he insisted.

'You may know a great deal, Mr Anderson, Richard!' she added. 'But there are some things about these parts that you know nothing about.'

Chapter 6

'Great news,' said the Widow O'Halloran as she hurried into her cottage.

Richard looked up from the table where he was sitting, writing some notes into a book. She was waving a piece of paper like a flag.

'What is it?' His curiosity was aroused.

'Well I was up at Johnny Mack's,' she said excitedly, 'and getting a few bits and pieces when he produced a letter for me from the top shelf. I knew immediately who it was from by the writing.' She put the letter under his nose. 'It's from my nephew Danny O'Sullivan,' she said proudly. 'Now would you be so kind as to read it for me?'

Richard wondered why, if she couldn't read it, she didn't ask someone in the shebeen to do so.

'I know what you are thinking,' she said. 'You're wondering why I didn't ask Johnny Mack to read it for me.' He smiled. 'Well the reason is, they are all so nosy the whole village would know the contents of my letter before milking time. I usually get young Sinéad to read my letters for me and she writes them for me as well.' She crossed her arms and sat back in the chair. 'Well...?' she nodded at him to read the letter.

Dear Aunt Margaret, I hope this letter finds you well — 'ah isn't he a thoughtful nephew?' she interjected. *We were all delighted to receive your correspondence recently.* She smiled proudly. 'I corresponded with him.' *All the family are well. There has been a great deal of unrest in Dublin recently, but I'll tell you more about that when I see you. I will be arriving in Galway city on Saturday afternoon. If you could manage to meet me at Eyre Square, that would be great if not I'll make my way out to your place (hopefully) before nightfall. Your nephew, Danny*

'Isn't that just grand,' she beamed. 'I haven't seen young Danny in over a year. I'm so looking forward to seeing him again.'

*   *   *   *

'God bless you, Miss,' said the travellers to Sinéad as they took the plateful of potato cakes and fried eggs. They sat outside the cottage and began to tuck into their food. Billy Keogh threw them a glance.

'All finished,' said the older traveller, wiping some of the egg from his long, flowing, white beard.

'Good,' said Keogh as he reached into his pocket and took out his purse. He handed the man some money.

'The blessings of God on you,' said the traveller as he quickly put the money into his jacket pocket.

'I hope it works,' Keogh snapped.

'You haven't had any trouble with the last poitín still,' the young man grinned as he gulped down some of the clear liquid from a bottle.

'I hear you make the finest poitín in these parts,' said the older one.

'Well that's true,' Billy Keogh sniggered. 'Thank you Martin, and you too John Joe. I'll no doubt see you below in the shebeen tonight.'

'Oh you will, to be sure,' said Martin. 'You have a grand daughter in Sinéad. She reminds me of your wife, Lord rest her.'

Billy Keogh just stared skywards. 'I'm going in for my dinner, if there's any left,' he snapped, and abruptly went inside.

'Where's my dinner?' he growled at Sinéad.

'Here Daddy.' She took it from the hearth. 'I was just keeping it warm.'

'You don't have to go feeding everyone who does a bit of work for me, I pay them all well enough.'

Sinéad didn't reply but put some tea down beside his meal.

'You know I only drink tea in the morning. God knows I've told you that often enough. Bring me over a couple of bottles of porter and be quick about it.' Sinéad did so. 'Now, sit down,' he commanded. 'You're always moving around the house like a frightened rabbit.'

Sinéad tied back her hair and, sitting near him, said brightly, 'The Widow O'Halloran's nephew is coming to visit on Saturday from Dublin.' He just grunted at her. 'She hasn't seen him for over a year, not since the time she went to Dublin for the wedding of her niece.'

Billy Keogh finished eating and opened the bottle of porter. 'Do you remember Danny?'

He looked at her. 'I remember some wiry, pale-faced runt of a thing that came to visit her five or six years ago.'

'Seven,' said Sinéad and smiled. 'Remember, Daddy, we fell into the bog hole.'

'I do,' he snapped. 'You were lucky it wasn't deeper; you would have gone the way your mother did, to a watery grave.'

Sinéad was amazed. This was the first time he'd mentioned her mother without being asked. She took courage from this and asked him about her. He sighed hard, then said, 'You are the spit of her. Those eyes, that transparent skin. The way—' he stopped himself. 'She's dead; talking about her won't bring her back.'

'I need to know, I have a right to know,' she insisted.

He flared, 'She drowned in an accident. That's all there is to it. No amount of talk is going to change the past. She's dead and gone.' He got up from the table and stormed out of the cottage.

Chapter 7

'Will you put your hands together and give a big, warm welcome to Martin and John Joe O'Driscoll, two of the finest musicians you're ever likely to meet in these parts,' Johnny Mack said proudly.

There was loud applause. Martin began to tune up on the uileann pipes. John Joe started warming up the tin whistle. They played several tunes. The Widow Fitzsimon, sitting by the fireside, broke into song after a little coaxing and sang a sad lament called 'As I roved out'. John Joe took up a fiddle while his father now played the concertina.

'They can play any instrument,' said Johnny Mack to his daughter Ciara.

They played some jigs and reels. This got a few of the girls out dancing. There was loud clapping and words of encouragement. Sinéad arrived in with her father and she looked around for the Widow O'Halloran. Her father ordered some drinks and a glass of raspberry for Sinéad. He headed over to Dingy O'Rourke.

Richard Anderson arrived into the shebeen. The widow waved furiously at him and he made his way over to her.

'That's the artist fella who is buying McMahons' old place,' whispered Dingy O'Rourke.

Billy Keogh looked at him in disbelief.

'That's only a shell of a place, only fit for the swallows to rest there,' he retorted.

'Well, it will soon be getting a new roof on it and that's a fact. I heard it from Dermot McGrath who sold him the place,' said Dingy.

'McGrath is as cute as they come, to convince someone to buy that place,' said Billy.

'Oh it wasn't his idea at all, it was the Widow O'Halloran who told him this gentleman from London wanted a place.'

'What's her game?' Billy Keogh wondered.

'I don't know,' said Dingy. 'But he's lodging in her house at present.'

'Did nobody warn him about that oul' Tartar!'

'Oh he seems to be getting on with her like a house on fire,' said Dingy. 'Sure look at him running about like a lap dog buying her drink.'

'Well, he's the bigger fool,' Billy Keogh grumbled.

'Good evening to you, sir,' said Johnny Mack to Richard as he approached the bar. 'Is the widow looking after you all right?' he laughed.

'Yes,' smiled Richard.

'She'd organise the good Lord himself.'

'I bought the derelict cottage,' said Richard.

'So I hear,' said Johnny Mack. 'News travels fast around here,' he grinned broadly and winked at him. 'Oh speaking of news . . . a parcel of newspapers was delivered for you.'

'Oh yes, my father does that to keep me informed,' grinned Richard. 'He's worried that his thirty-eight-year-old son might not be up to date with current affairs.' He returned to the widow with the drinks and the parcel of newspapers.

'Well I never,' said the widow. 'All those papers for you.'

'My father's idea. He used to send them to me in Africa as well.'

Sinéad looked in amazement at the bundle. There was a lull in the music while the musicians got themselves something to drink.

'Would you ever read us something out of the papers there?' said the widow. 'Sure we're starved for news around here.'

'I will,' said Richard smiling at Sinéad.

The Widow O'Halloran stood up.

'Quiet down now everyone, Mr Anderson here is going to read us some news from the papers beside him sent to him by his father in London.'

'I meant later,' said Richard a little embarrassed.

'That's a wonderful idea,' said Johnny Mack. 'We're all ears.'

'This should be good,' said Peadar Walsh.

Richard Anderson opened the parcel of papers, some of which were dated two months earlier, and peered at the crowd. They were waiting and watching with great expectation. His eyes widened as he read aloud the headlines from the *London Times*.

'*Europe mobilises for war.*'

There was a deadly silence from the villagers.

'Go on', said the widow coaxing him.

'*Opinions are sharply divided about Great Britain entering this conflict. Pro–war supporters say it will be a purifying agent and root out the evil symptoms that produce national decadence around Europe. Military rather than diplomatic solutions are the only answer, and that if Great Britain entered the conflict, the war would be short and a swift victory assured for the Allied forces.*'

'Who's fighting who?' asked Kevin Nolan.

Richard scanned the paper. 'It seems Russia, France and Great Britain are all against Germany and the Austro-Hungarian Empire.'

Richard picked up another paper. The headline read: '*World on a collision course. German troops estimated at over four million strong.*'

Another paper's headline read: '*The spark that ignited the powder keg.*'

The widow crossed herself. 'Jesus, Mary and holy St Joseph, this is terrible! Please continue,' she insisted.

He picked up an earlier paper and read loudly: '*On Monday 28th June 1914, Archduke Franz Ferdinand, heir to the Austrian throne, and his wife Sophie were assassinated in Sarajevo, the capital of Bosnia, which was taken over by Austria-Hungary in 1908. Police suspect a secret terrorist group called the Black Hand which operates out of Serbia.*' He read the sub-headings:

'*Austria-Hungary declares war on Serbia. Czar Nicholas II orders Russian mobilisation in support of the Serbs. August 1st Germany declares war on Russia.*'

Richard picked up another paper. He could hardly believe what he was reading. '*War clouds gather.*' Another headline in large black print: '*August 3rd Germany declares war on France. August 4th German troops invade Belgium. Threats to the Channel ports and the invasion of Belgium by German troops leave Great Britain no other choice but to declare war on Germany on August 4th (11pm London time).*'

Richard read some more headlines but was becoming more and more depressed by each one he glanced at: '*German troops sweep through Belgium. German troops take Brussels on the 20th August. Destruction of property and execution of civilians is German policy says Belgian politician.*'

A sub-headline read:

'*Louvain famous library of priceless medieval manuscripts burned by German troops.*'

'*At Morhange, French infantry suffer enormous casualties against German advances. Modern artillery and well-positioned machine guns give the German troops a decided advantage. Great*

Britain's first battle in Europe since Waterloo. Troops on both sides of the divide share the hardship, hunger and fatigue of war.'

'I think we've heard enough thanks, Richard,' the Widow O'Halloran sighed. 'Here we are not long into the new God-given century and they're spoiling it already by sending those poor young men to their deaths. Sure aren't they all some mother's son or husband or brother. That's war for you,' she said sadly as she finished her glass of porter.

'Thank you very much, Mr Anderson,' said Johnny Mack. 'Frightening news indeed,' he said nervously. 'Perhaps Martin and John Joe will lift our spirits with a few more songs.'

'We will to be sure,' said Martin.

'And with the help of God,' continued Johnny Mack, 'war will not touch our shores. Let's hope it ends shortly.'

Martin addressed the crowd then.

'This is a piece of music I collected, called the Two Magicians.'

'Work your magic,' said the Widow O'Halloran as the musicians began to play.

Chapter 8

Seventeen years earlier

'You're a washout,' shouted Willie Keogh to his son. 'A washout!'

Billy Keogh and his father had been clearing rocks from a field all morning. There was always tension when they were together which sometimes broke out into conflict, usually verbal and sometimes physical.

The talk came round to the way he was treating his wife Sylvia.

'You want to cop on to yourself, young laddie. Treat her with a bit of respect. You're always growling at her like some bear with a sore paw.'

'You can talk,' snapped Billy.

'What's that supposed to mean?' yelled his father, pulling himself up to all of his six feet three inches height. He stood strong, fists clenched.

'I saw you, with your shouting and roaring.'

'It was never at her,' Willie snapped. 'It was at life. Or the way you behaved. I loved my dear Bridie and there's not a day passes that I don't miss her company. When the sea took her and your brother Michael my heart was broken.'

'We all suffered,' growled Billy.

'They're dead these four years and that's a fact, nothing could prevent what happened. A freak storm and eleven good people lose their lives.' Willie Keogh let his hands relax and he raised them towards the sky in a ritualistic fashion as if pleading with the elements to make sense of what happened on that awful day.

'Prayer won't bring them back,' said Billy as he put on his jacket and picked up the spade.

Willie Keogh as if coming out of a trance turned and stared at his son. 'You see those stones in this field?' Billy just stared at him. 'Your heart is as hard as them and I don't know why it should be so,' his eyes pleaded with his son. 'What is it, son? Why can you not realise what you have in that lovely young woman?'

Sylvia came out of the cottage.

'Dinner's ready!' she called. The two men walked silently back to the cottage.

'Bedad that smells good,' said Willie removing his cap.

'Come on Father, wash your hands first. You too Billy.'

'Yes, boss,' Willie chuckled. 'These young ladies nowadays take no nonsense. What's for dinner?' he asked warmly.

'Beef, braised with onions, carrots and porter. First some leek and oatmeal soup.'

'A feast fit for a king,' said Willie.

Billy sat down.

'I don't want soup!' He cut himself a slice of soda bread. Sylvia wiped her brow and placed a plate of food in front of him. He dipped the bread into the gravy and began to eat.

'That soup is only gorgeous,' said Willie.

'How are you getting on removing the stones?' Sylvia asked.

'Oh it's hard work . . . the weight of some of them would kill you,' sighed Willie.

'It's the only thing that grows in those fields,' grumbled Billy. 'No wonder Cromwell sent the poor people to Connaught.'

'I might be able to get a loan of a horse from Tim Kelly . . .'

'We should buy a horse,' said Billy. 'We need one, and a cart or a jaunting car.'

'And where do you think we could get the money for them?'

asked his father. 'Are you hoping to find a crock of gold under some of those boulders or what?'

'I have ways,' said Billy.

'How?' he asked.

'Well, for one thing a poitín still. Sell the bottles at the fair, word would get around and before we'd know it, we could afford a horse and anything else we wanted.'

'You'll have the peelers down on us like a ton of bricks or maybe the army itself.'

'To hell with the peelers and the army . . . besides, they have more important things to worry about with the Fenians* than some poor farmer trying to scratch out a living in this hovel.'

'This is no hovel,' said Willie showing his annoyance.

Sylvia produced the dinner for herself and Willie and handed her husband a dish of Ocean Swell**.

'This house is a home. Your mother loved it and kept it as clean as any fancy house you'd find in the city.'

'You were never in any fancy house in any city,' Billy retorted. Sylvia rubbed her stomach. Billy stared at her. 'Are you all right?'

'Yes,' she smiled. 'The baby is kicking.'

'I hope it's a boy,' said Billy. 'We could do with an extra pair of strong arms around here.'

'The Widow O'Halloran thinks it's going to be a girl.' She smiled with her eyes.

'Why do you go near that nosy hag? All she wants is to say she helped deliver every child in the village; she thinks that will be her passport to heaven.'

'The Widow O'Halloran is a fine woman and a caring one,' said Willie.

*Fenians: revolutionaries who sought Irish independence.
**Ocean Swell: a dish of carrageen seaweed cooked in milk and sugar.

'Well I don't want you with her.' He looked hard at his young wife.

'If you need help I will ask Mary Scanlon, the butcher's wife; she has eleven of her own.'

Sylvia got up and brought back some dessert to Willie. She picked up her shawl.

'I'm going out for a walk.'

They watched her head out the door and up the narrow path towards the bog.

'You don't know how lucky you are having such a lovely, sweet young wife like Sylvia. It puzzles me how a young girl from Brittany would be willing to spend her life looking after two cranky things like us. She's so refined and delicate, almost like a piece of bone china. Are you listening to me at all?' Willie pleaded to his son.

'Don't tell me how to treat my wife,' Billy snapped.

Willie got up and stretched. 'I don't know where you got your anger from but it will eat away at you like a worm would eat into an apple. You mark my words.' Willie headed over to the bed. 'We've done enough for today. I'm going to take a little rest, for I'm worn out.'

Billy just sat silently staring at the wall. When his father began to snore he rose from the table, grabbed his jacket and cap and headed out.

He walked down the road towards the great solitude of the cliffs. There he could sit and plan his future. He would need more money, for as soon as one child arrived more would surely follow. Some of the women here were like breeding machines, he said to himself. As he walked the cliffs he was stopped in his tracks by a riveting sight. There was his wife swimming in the sea! Billy couldn't believe his eyes. She was surrounded by a pod of dolphins. Her laughter echoed up the cliffs. She was swimming as strongly and beautifully as the dolphins.

He was furious. Had she no shame, swimming about in all her nakedness with those wild creatures? He hurried down towards the shore and hid behind a large boulder watching them frolicking about. She seemed as wild as the creatures that swam with her.

He stood motionless with a wild glare in his eyes. He knew Sylvia loved the sea and he was aware she often slipped away to go for long swims. She appeared to have no sense of danger from the sea or the creatures that lived there. Perhaps she was bewitched. There was a strangeness about her at times. He had noticed it. He was almost convinced she was a sea spirit; she certainly seemed like one now.

She had more or less admitted it to him when they first got married. 'There is a great hunger in me for the unusual. The sea calls me like a friend,' she'd said to him. He remembered the first time he had seen her slip away after supper saying she needed some fresh air.

He had followed her for he was very jealous and couldn't help himself. Here he had the most beautiful woman he had ever laid eyes on, now his young bride. He was afraid some of the other village bucks might try to make advances towards her. He had watched her in the failing light heading down to the beach and slipping into the dark waters. She seemed to be spurred on by some fixation of her imagination.

He felt so uncertain of her, yet she never gave him any reason to doubt her love for him. She thought by starting a family it might bring him a calmness and a serenity, but it didn't seem to be happening. He was as tense and angry as ever.

Billy Keogh watched her swimming with the dolphins for a long time. What all this was about he just couldn't fathom. Was this some fulfilment of a private dream of hers, to make contact with these strange sea creatures? She seemed to be so in tune with their environment.

When Sylvia finally arrived back to the cottage that evening he challenged her about it. His father had gone down to the shebeen so there was no one to interfere. As she entered the darkened cottage, he swung out with his right hand and slapped her hard across the face.

With her pale green eyes gleaming by the fire light she stared silently back at him. 'I saw you!' he shouted, 'swimming around with those creatures.'

Sylvia just stood in silence, her body trembling.

'I know it's not the first time – you're out in the sea any time my back is turned.' Their eyes locked. He turned away from her and went to the fireplace. He bent down and piled some turf on the fire.

She moved slowly over to him and laid her hands gently on his shoulder. 'Billy, don't be angry with me when I go to the sea shore. You see, I can hear the sea call. There is a murmur in the sea . . . it's ever so gentle, but when I listen I imagine I hear my name being called. I feel at one with the water. I can't explain, my love, but it's something beyond my grasp. It's still unknowable, yet I sense I'm part of it. When I'm in the water swimming with the gentle dolphins I feel part of the ocean like the wind and the waves. The dolphins feel like they are family. Does that seem so terribly strange, Billy?'

He shrugged her arms from his shoulders and headed out the door. Then turning he stared at her, framed against the doorway.

'Yes, it seems strange to me,' he shouted. 'You're either mad or some kind of freak.' She began to weep. 'I'm going down to join the oul' fella in Johnny Mack's. Come down if you wish, only my breeches need mending so sew them first. If you do call in, keep your tongue harnessed about the sea and those weird creature friends of yours.'

*   *   *   *

Later, Sylvia made her way down to the shebeen.

'Come in,' shouted Johnny Mack as he spied her at the doorway. 'There's great music tonight,' he said cheerfully.

'God save all here,' said Sylvia and the villagers looked over at her.

'Come, sit beside me,' said the Widow O'Halloran who was up near the fireside.

Sylvia threw a glance at her husband and her father-in-law who were in heavy discussion with three other men. Billy looked hard at her then turned back to engage in the argument.

The widow eyed Sylvia and could see a slight bruising on her cheek. 'What happened to you, child? Don't tell me it was that blackguard. What in the name of God is wrong with him?'

'It was my fault,' said Sylvia. 'I upset him.'

'He's no right to lay a hand in violence against an angel like you, my dear. I've a good mind to give him a piece of my mind.'

'No don't,' said Sylvia. 'I'm all right.'

'And you with child, full with life inside you. To dare strike you.'

'He's so unhappy all the time.' Sylvia began to weep. 'It's my fault.'

'Nonsense child. There are some people who block out happiness, who only seem content when they're miserable, and try to make everyone they come in contact with the same. They're like vampires, God forgive me for saying it, sucking the joy out of others.'

Johnny Mack brought over a glass of wine to Sylvia. 'It's French, the wine,' he said brightly. 'I thought you might like some.'

'Thank you,' she smiled warmly.

'There's a catch,' he winked. 'We'd love you to give us a song before the musicians start up again.'

'Ah not tonight she's a little upset,' said the widow.

'It's fine,' said Sylvia. 'How could I refuse after this?' She sipped the red wine.

'Quiet now, ladies and gentlemen, for the lovely Sylvia Keogh is going to sing for us. Then we'll have our friends from the county Sligo play for us again.' There was loud applause.

'The song I will sing for you is a shepherd's song from the Auvergne region in France.'

Sylvia took a breath, closed her eyes and sang the love song.

'She has the voice and looks of an angel,' said Willie Keogh as tears welled up in his eyes.

*   *   *   *

Early next morning Sylvia awoke with a start. She had terrible dreams all night, that the sea was stained with blood. The rain lashed at the window pane and the window frame rattled. Billy was not to be seen. She quickly got dressed, then to her horror she saw the pikestaff was gone from above the fireplace. The cottage door was wide open to the elements. A pool of water was on the flagstones. Sylvia looked out but could not see her husband anywhere. Then it began to dawn on her what he was about to do. Unconsciously she rubbed her swollen belly.

Grabbing her shawl she ran out into the driving rain. Her tears mingled with the rain that beat at her. Across the soggy bog she ran wildly. Her heart pounded in her chest.

'Billy!' She shrieked. 'Billy! Where are you?' She made her way towards the cliffs. She hoped to God she wasn't too late.

Huge waves rolled in from the sea breaking against the cliffs.

'Billy!' she called again. She was now soaked to the skin. Her shawl had slipped from her head and her hair was matted against her face. She headed along the cliff face and looked towards the beach. There was still no sign of her husband.

Mobbing clouds of sea gulls screamed overhead, having been driven in to the shore by the violent storms. The sea seemed to boil in rage. It was violent and unpredictable.

'Where are you?' she cried. 'Please don't do anything foolish.'

She decided then to go to the blowhole for if he was there he could be easily concealed. She ran awkwardly down the slippery wet tufts of grass.

*   *   *   *

Billy Keogh had an idea that the dolphins used the blowhole to rest in at certain times. He had seen them leave there in the early light, on occasion. His guess was right. They had made their way into the long tunnel. And he knew that when they passed out the narrow entrance, he would get at least one of them, probably two. They were dumb animals after all, they wouldn't suspect a thing, he convinced himself.

Sylvia stopped suddenly. She could see her husband hanging over the blowhole like some giant crab. He held the long pikestaff ready to take aim.

'Billy! Billy!' She screamed. He took no notice. He was in such a very precarious position that if he lost his grip he was gone. Sylvia knew he couldn't swim – like most of the villagers.

'Billy!' She realised what he was trying to do: to kill the dolphins.

In single file they began to leave the underwater cave. They seemed not to sense the danger awaiting them. As the first dolphin passed out into the open sea, Billy Keogh took the opportunity to strike at it.

Sylvia carefully climbed down the slippery rocks towards her husband.

'Don't, Billy, for pity's sake.'

Gripping the pike with both hands he lunged for the first dolphin. There was a loud squealing sound as the metal spike pierced the flesh of the dolphin. Blood spurted out and the white foam turned red. He began to lose his footing. Sylvia moved as quick as she could across the slippery rocks and grabbed hold of his jacket and the belt on his trousers. With all her strength she pulled him back from falling to his death. The rain beat down; they stared at each other.

'Stop, for heaven's sake! Are you mad?'

He yelled, 'Get back to the cottage!'

The dolphins swam about in panic. They made loud clicking sounds and slapped the water with their tails in anger and sorrow. The wounded dolphin jerked its body in pain. Billy Keogh struck again with the pikestaff piercing another dolphin.

His wife pulled at him and grabbed the staff, trying to take it from him.

'You're killing them,' she cried.

'Leave me!' he growled, and pushed her away. She screamed helplessly. He turned but the rest of the pod were heading out to sea to safety. He stared after them, watching as they tried to support the wounded dolphins with their own bodies, stroking them with their flippers to comfort them.

'Good riddance!' he yelled after them. He looked down at the crimson pool below knowing that he must have mortally wounded two of them.

Raising the pikestaff above his head in triumph he yelled out in victory. 'They'll think twice before coming around here again and if they do I'll be waiting for them.' He turned to his wife but she was nowhere to be seen.

In a panic he called her name but there was no answer. He looked to the water but she was not there. Visibility was poor and the rain continued to pelt down. He stood staring for a long time. She's probably gone back to the cottage or to that oul' biddy the Widow O'Halloran, he said to himself. He knew she could move fast, even in her condition. She had the grace and speed of a hare at times. She was probably telling his old man by now the terrible things he'd done to the dolphins. Billy Keogh was only sorry he didn't get them all.

He carefully made his way along the narrow edge to the safety of the rocks then up to the lower part of the cliffs. He began to feel very cold and chilled, his body trembling as he made his way slowly across the bog to the cottage. As he entered the cottage a warm fire welcomed him. The steam began to rise from his clothes. He was glad to be out of that weather. Replacing the pikestaff on the wall, he got himself a bottle of porter, and stood in front of the fire.

'That's a shocking day,' said his father as he entered the cottage carrying eggs in his hands. He placed them in a bowl and took off his hat and jacket.

'You'll get your end in those sopping clothes,' he said to his son. 'Take them off and I'll heat up some of that soup for you.'

Billy went and changed his clothes. Then he came back and sat at the table supping from the bottle of porter.

'I hope Sylvia isn't out in that,' said Willie.

There was no response from his son.

'You were out at the crack of dawn this morning – and in

that weather. Why was that?' his father enquired. Billy remained silent. 'Oh be like that,' said the father. 'I'll peel a few potatoes for dinner. It's the least I might do, with young Sylvia carrying a child.'

He first heated the soup and gave it to his son with some bread. Then he started to peel the potatoes. He began singing *'Oh the praties they grow small over here, oh the praties they grow small over here . . .'*

Chapter 9

'Father Darcy, Father Darcy . . .' the widow called to the priest as he stood chatting to Tom Ward who was just about to mount his horse.

'Good morning, Widow O'Halloran. You look in a bit of a hurry.'

The widow was panting hard. 'I called to the chapel, Father. I thought I might find you there.'

'What's on your mind?' the priest enquired.

She looked hard at Tom Ward.

'I get the message,' Tom grinned. 'You want to talk in private. Call around tonight, Father, for dinner.'

'I will, thank you, Tom. At about seven o'clock.' The priest turned and began to walk briskly towards his house. The widow hurried alongside him. 'Well, Margaret, what's on your mind?'

'Well Father, if you'd slow up I might be able to get my breath and tell you.' He stopped and stared at her.

'Now what is it?' Before she could answer he told her he had to write an urgent letter to the bishop and wanted it to go to Galway city today. Johnny Mack said he would bring it, sure he was heading there at midday. Father Darcy knew if he got stuck with the widow she would take up his whole morning, all day if she had her way.

'Could we go and talk over a cup of tea? I've a terrible dryness in my throat.'

'Oh very well,' he sighed. 'We're near the house. But Margaret – it will have to be brief. I must get this letter away.'

They sat in his parlour and had some boiled cake and tea.

'Well, are you going to keep me in suspense all morning?'

'Well now Father, you're going to think me very odd what I'm about to tell you . . .'

'Nothing anyone says around here could shock me so let's hear it.'

'Father Darcy, I heard the banshee last night.'

'Now, Margaret, what's a good Catholic woman like yourself doing believing in such things?'

'It's true father as sure as I'm sitting here.'

'It was probably a vixen.' He looked skywards. 'Now, if that's what sent you haring out of your home this morning, then I'm very surprised at you.'

'There's more, Father! I had the most awful dream last night, it was concerning young Sylvia Keogh. She was calling for help.'

'Don't alarm yourself, my good woman. If something was up I'd be the first to know.' Then he said teasingly, 'I don't suppose you were down at Johnny Mack's last night drinking his strong whiskey?'

'Father, you know me.'

'I know you Margaret. You're a good woman, but I hear you're a little too fond of *uisce beatha*.'

'It's only to keep the chilly winds out,' she retorted.

Suddenly there was loud pounding on the door.

'Who in the name of God is that?' The priest opened the door.

Willie Keogh stood trembling.

'Come quickly Father, it's poor Sylvia.'

The three of them hurried down the road.

'What is it?' asked Father Darcy trying to keep up with the old man. There was a look of wild madness in his eyes as he beckoned the priest onwards. They turned up a boreen and took a short cut across the bog, then down to the beach.

Gulls wheeled in the air. The sea was calm. Along the strand stood Billy Keogh as still as stone.

Father Darcy could see two dead dolphins lying on the beach. The mobbing clouds of sea birds overhead circled in frenzied excitement. The gulls had already done their work, taking huge chunks of flesh out of the dead carcases.

As they approached, the widow yelled, 'Oh Mother of God!' when she saw the still form of Sylvia lying face down in the sand. The widow let out another loud cry of sorrow as she looked at the young woman's body wreathed in seaweed.

'My poor child, my poor child.' She cradled the lifeless body. 'Who did this to you, child? You poor crathur.' She sobbed and wailed.

'It was an accident,' said Billy Keogh staring out to sea.

'When she didn't come home last night we went searching for her,' said Willie his eyes red with tears. 'We looked along the cliffs and the rocks then—'

'Then what?' asked the priest.

'Then we saw them, the dolphins. They seemed to be pushing something towards the shore.' He cried as he related how the dolphins had brought Sylvia's body back to the land and stayed offshore until the tide washed her up on the dry land. Then they'd turned and moved away.

'That was a bad storm yesterday. Surely Sylvia wasn't out swimming in those seas? Sure it took the life of these two wild creatures who are used to it; what chance would she have?'

'It wasn't the sea killed the dolphins, it was me,' said Billy.

'Sweet Mary, Mother of God!' exclaimed the widow as she lay with her head on the young girl's body. 'The child within her is still alive. It's a miracle, praise the Lord!'

'Praise the Lord!' said Father Darcy as he crossed himself.

Chapter 10

'God doesn't close one door but He opens another,' said the Widow O'Halloran rocking the baby girl from side to side. 'Have you ever seen a more beautiful child? You're a little dote, aren't you?' The widow smiled down at the baby.

'Sinéad is a fine name, Willie,' said Father Darcy.

'Well, my dear departed wife would have approved. She loved Irish girls' names. That was a lovely funeral service for dear Sylvia,' said Willie.

'May God in his good mercy look kindly on her soul,' said Father Darcy.

Billy stood looking at his new daughter. He rubbed his face hard.

'How am I supposed to look after a tiny child like that and try to run this bit of a farm?'

'Don't worry, Billy,' said the widow. 'I'll take the child for a time, it's the least I can do. Sylvia was always so good and decent to me. I'll ask Mrs Fitzgerald to be a wet nurse for a few weeks. She has a young baby herself, about three months old. She's a big hearted woman and the babies would be grand company for each other.'

'Well, that's all settled,' said Father Darcy. 'I'd better get back. We'll baptise the child after Sunday Mass if that suits.'

'Thank you again, Father, for your kindness,' said Willie, shaking the priest's hand.

As the priest began to leave the cottage he saw several villagers heading towards the cottage. Their faces wore a cold expression and they moved like a mob.

'What do they want?' asked the widow.

'They don't look like they're coming to pay their respects,' said Willie.

The priest stood like someone ready to do battle. 'What's up?' he addressed the crowd.

'Well, Father Darcy,' said one of the younger men speaking for the others. 'We've been thinking—'

'Yes,' snapped the priest as if he knew what they were about to say.

'Well . . .' said the young man awkwardly, 'We're sorry for your troubles, Billy, but it isn't natural what happened, that a child could survive the cold water of the sea like that and the way those big fish brought the body to shore . . .'

The widow handed the child to Willie and brushed past the priest and locked eyes with the young man. 'What are you saying, Finbar O'Brien?'

'I'm saying we think she's a changeling, a fairy child, and it's best if we put her back in the sea.'

'She's my child,' shouted Billy Keogh. 'No one touches her.'

The widow prodded O'Brien with her finger. 'You go near that child over my dead body.'

'If anyone so much as touches a hair on the head of my granddaughter,' bellowed Willie, 'I'll take my pikestaff to them.'

'Well, you've heard the family,' said the priest, 'And if you don't leave right now I'll get on to the bishop and have you all excommunicated. You know what that means. You'll meet your maker on the day of Judgement already damned to the fires of hell.'

The crowd began slowly to disband and melt away like the morning mist. Young baby Sinéad began to cry softly in her grandfather's arms.

Chapter 11

The train puffed and steamed its way into Galway station. The Widow O'Halloran pushed her way through the milling crowds.

'Follow me,' she said to Richard and Sinéad as she got as near to the platform as possible.

Black smoke billowed around the station and tiny particles of soot fell like black snowflakes from the clouds of smoke. The doors swung out from the carriages and people began to pile out from the train.

The widow's eyes scanned the crowd. She could hardly contain her excitement. Her favourite nephew was coming to visit; she hoped he would stay for a long time. As people filed past she could not see any sign of him. She hoped he hadn't missed the train, or perhaps it had been full – would he have had to wait until another day?

By now nearly all the passengers had left the train to be greeted by overjoyed relatives and friends. A feeling of disappointment began to creep over the old woman. Then her eyes widened. There he was, holding a large cardboard box and struggling to get out the door of the carriage onto the platform.

'Danny!' she cried.

Danny carefully placed the large box on the ground and rushed to her. He grabbed her by the waist and swung her around in a complete circle.

'Put me down,' she laughed, kicking her legs furiously.

'You'll kill yourself with the weight of me.' She cupped his face with her hands and gave him a big kiss. 'God bless you Danny boy, for coming to visit your old aunt.'

'Ah, sure I'd nothing better to do,' he grinned. 'Just kidding. It's great to be here,' he said brightly. He took off his cap and shoved it into the pocket of his brown woollen jacket.

'You've turned into a fine, handsome young man,' she said, eyeing him up and down.

'Oh you're only saying that because it's true,' he laughed.

Tears began to escape from her eyes. She wiped them with the back of her hand then brought him over to Sinéad and Richard.

'This is my nephew, Danny O'Sullivan,' she said proudly. She introduced Richard to him. They shook hands warmly.

'So this is Sinéad Keogh?' He could not believe how beautiful she had become.

'Hello, Danny.' She smiled with her eyes.

'Richard here was good enough to hire a jaunting car to

bring us to the city and back home,' said the widow, linking arms with her nephew.

They began to walk out of the station, then Danny stopped.

'I'd forget my head only it's attached.' He hurried back for the cardboard box.

They went into Eyre Square and Richard suggested they should go for a meal.

'Great idea,' said Danny. 'I'm so hungry I could eat the leg of a table,' he joked.

There was a vibrancy in the city that Sinéad always enjoyed. It was market day and there were so many different sounds and smells. Music filled the air as travelling musicians played on street corners. Sinéad could not get over the sense of colour there was in the city. The shops and the market had a wonderful variety of colourful things for sale. Some of the younger women and men wore bright clothes; the only colour Sinéad saw in her village was on the birds or the bushes, the furze and heather.

She enjoyed being in the city which was so alive that even the dogs and pigeons made it their own. Horses and motorcars all added to the strange but exciting sounds. It seemed so loud to Sinéad, but the people that passed them by didn't appear to notice or be bothered.

'Thank you for coming in to meet me,' said Danny to Sinéad.

'But I didn't come especially to meet you. The widow asked me to join her and Richard for the company.'

'Oh I see,' said Danny in mock disappointment.

'I mean I was delighted to come and see you,' said Sinéad.

'Hold this please.' Danny handed Richard the cardboard box and ran over to a stall, bought a sprig of flowers and a straw hat with a wide brim, dressed with cloth flowers and a red velvet ribbon. He returned quickly, made a big gesture and handed the widow the flowers. Then he placed the hat on Sinéad's head. They laughed at each other.

'Shall we try here for something to eat?' suggested Richard. 'I've been in here before, it's very good indeed.'

They entered the Wishbone Restaurant.

'What a fancy place!' said the widow as she looked at the people dining at the different tables. The tables were covered in white cotton tablecloths with a small vase of flowers placed in the centre of each one. Heads turned as they entered. They were seated by the manager at a window where they could watch the passers-by.

A menu was produced.

'You better read it for me,' said the widow, 'you people with your fancy education,' she teased.

'That hat suits you,' said Danny to Sinéad.

'Thank you,' she replied. 'It was very kind of you.'

She removed the hat and placed it on the window sill. Richard put on his glasses and read the menu out loud.

'Creamed fresh haddock.'

'Creamed fresh haddock . . .' the widow repeated after him.

'It's in a mustard sauce,' said Richard. 'Trout baked in wine, stuffed pork steaks, braised beef, wild duck – widgeon or mallard, Irish stew—'

'That's for me,' interrupted the widow.

He continued, 'And spiced tongue.'

'Have they no boxty?' asked Danny teasing.

'What's that?' asked Sinéad.

'You've never heard of boxty?' He went into a verse of *boxty in the griddle, boxty in the pan, if you don't eat boxty, you'll never get your man*. He laughed winking at Sinéad. 'It's potatoes, flour, bacon fat and butter,' he explained.

'I'll try the stuffed pork,' said Sinéad.

'I'll have the braised beef,' said Danny.

Richard ordered the trout. The others had a starter of cockle soup while Sinéad had the potato soup.

'This is the life,' said Danny as he cut into the beef. 'Good food, good company, what more could a man ask for?' he beamed. 'One should give oneself a little gift every day. It could be a new bar of soap, an extra cup of tea, a newspaper, perhaps a kiss from a pretty girl,' he looked at Sinéad.

'You mean, know how to spoil yourself,' said the widow.

'Ah now, Auntie Maggie you wouldn't object to a few things like that.'

'Don't mind him, Sinéad. These young Dubs are getting mighty forward with their tongues.'

'Ah now, that's not fair,' he responded. 'Nowadays the poor people are so downtrodden they're afraid to even dream in case they're taxed for it or accused of sinning.' His tone had become more serious.

'How are things in Dublin?' asked Richard.

'Ah poor old Dublin, as my father says, is in a state of chassis. With the death of poor Parnell in 1891 things have never been the same.'

'What do you think?' asked Richard.

'Well, I don't know what things are like in London, but Dublin has one of the most underfed populations in Europe with Moscow a close second. The worst housing and the worst paid. The highest death rate of any other European city.'

'You're not serious,' said the widow.

'I'm afraid I am. Don't get me wrong, there's a lot of wealth as well. There are the haves and the have nots. Big Jim Larkin and James Connolly tried to do something about it. They organised a strike of the Irish Transport and General Workers Union. A bitter few months followed with William Murphy organising over four hundred employers to lock out workers who joined the union. Over 24,000 workers were locked out. There were massive rallies. The police were called in and there were deaths and injuries as a result of the baton charges. Some workers were arrested. Even Big Jim got imprisonment. The citizen army was formed to protect the strikers.

'On the political front, people are calling for Home Rule. Patrick Pearse gave a great speech in Sackville Street on the importance of Home Rule. Some members of the British Parliament are in favour of it.'

Sinéad was fascinated by Danny – he was so animated. As he talked, he would run his hands through his black, curly hair as if to hold back the thoughts that might burst out of the top of his head. Sinéad was not used to such enthusiasm about life among the people she knew. Most of the older people had resigned themselves to existing in life, as if their emotions and thoughts were trapped inside their bodies never to be released. Here was this young man who was like a steed with the wind in its nostrils, ready to gallop across the landscape of life.

He continued with the same excitement and authority.

'There are so many splinter groups – you have the Gaelic League, Sinn Féin, Michael Connolly's socialist movement, Cumann na nGael, the Irish Republican Brotherhood, the GAA, Irish Ireland, the Labour movement, the Irish Volunteers, the Citizen Army. Then in the North, the unionists are up in arms. They don't want Home Rule. Sir Edward Carson organised a mass meeting where nearly a quarter of a million Ulstermen signed a Solemn League and Covenant, not in ink but in blood, swearing to defeat Home Rule. They're getting themselves armed to the teeth. The Ulster Volunteer Force has been involved in gun running, getting 35,000 rifles and a million rounds of ammunition. When Dublin got wind that the loyalists were arming themselves, many flocked to the drill halls of the Irish Volunteers. They're not aiming to fight the North, nor are the unionists armed to fight us. They all want to fight the British Army on account of the Home Rule issue. Those for and those against. And to top it all, Europe has been plunged into war – with Englishmen, Irishmen, Ulstermen, Welsh and Scots all fighting together in the one army against the hun.'

'They're mad, every one of them,' said the widow. 'Nothing only bloodshed will come out of that. Some day they'll all have to live together and rebuild all they've destroyed. Not that you can bring back a life,' she sighed.

'I'm inclined to agree with you, Mrs O'Halloran,' said Richard.

'Call me Margaret or the Widow O'Halloran, and don't you be so formal.'

'Who'd fancy some coffee or tea?' asked Danny.

'Oh tea for me, you can't beat it,' said the widow. 'What's in the box that you're carrying around like gold?' she asked, giving her nephew a friendly nudge.

'Well it's from Ma and Da to you.' He put on a flat Dublin accent.

'Oh they shouldn't have. Danny's father is in the Royal Dublin Constabulary,' she told Richard. 'He gets a good wage. My younger sister Maura is the best you'll meet anywhere.'

'From good stock,' Danny teased.

'The finest,' the widow laughed as she opened the parcel. She chuckled as she took out a bonnet. 'That sister of mine. Does she think an oul' one like myself is going to walk around the village wearing that!' Then she took out a woollen blanket.

'Isn't that just lovely? That will keep me warm on these cold winter nights. My goodness! Biscuits, tea and sugar!' she exclaimed as she found the rest of the contents of the box.

'There's a letter for you as well.' He handed it over to her.

'Well, she's the kindest . . . I must get you to write me a letter, Sinéad.'

'I'll write it, if you like,' said Danny.

'No you won't,' said the widow. 'We women need to have some private words with each other, not for your eyes,' she retorted.

'That's great! I carry a heavy box all the way from Clontarf to Galway and that's the thanks I get,' he teased.

They spent most of the day walking around the city enjoying themselves, and taking in the sights. Finally it was time to leave. They sang and laughed all the way back to the village in the jaunting car. The widow beamed saying she hadn't enjoyed herself so much in years. Sinéad too could not remember a more enjoyable day out.

Chapter 12

When Sinéad arrived home she was surprised to see a motor car parked at the side of the cottage. She entered quietly. The conversation stopped as she came in, suspicious eyes staring hard at her. Her father sat at the table and was flanked by two men. They held a stillness as Sinéad moved into the centre of the room. Her eyes fixed on what was laid across the table. Carefully displayed was an army rifle, several hand guns with what looked like boxes of bullets, and six grenades together like eggs. Then she noticed a wad of money close to her father. He immediately covered it with his two hands. They locked eyes.

'You're late!' he said sourly. 'Go and make up some supper for our guests.'

Sinéad became aware of someone standing behind her. She could get the strong smell of stale tobacco from his clothes. One of the men stood up from the table, gave a small gesture and the man behind Sinéad backed out the door and lit up a cigarette.

'So you must be young Sinéad,' said the stranger.

Sinéad had no idea who they were or what they were doing in her home. She smiled awkwardly. He could see she was still staring at the guns.

'We live in troubled times, young lady.' He fingered a hand gun then picked it up as if to examine it.

'Go make something to eat and don't stand there all night like a dummy,' her father growled anxiously.

'Not for us, thanks, Billy laddy,' the stranger retorted. 'We're leaving, but we will take a bottle each of your excellent fire water,' he grinned. 'You did well, Billy,' he finished, patting him on the back. He nodded to the other men at the table who quickly took up several hessian sacks from under the table and placed the weapons and ammunition inside them. They brushed out past Sinéad not giving her a glance.

'Good night, Billy laddy, young Sinéad,' said the stranger as he picked up three bottles of the poitín and left.

Billy Keogh watched after the men, sitting motionless until he heard the sound of the car engine starting up. Lights pierced the darkness and the car moved quickly down the narrow road.

Sinéad hurried to make her father some supper, but as she passed by him he reached out and grabbed her wrist in a vice-like grip.

'You saw nothing here tonight! Understand? Nothing.' Sinéad nodded and he released his grip. She moved away.

*   *   *   *

After Sunday Mass Sinéad went to the cemetery and placed a sprig of heather on her mother's and grandfather's graves. She missed her grandfather so much. When Willie was alive there had been laughter in the cottage. Sinéad remembered fondly how he would make her wooden toys, take her for walks or bring her home a present after visiting a market or fair.

A wren showed briefly on a tombstone, then flew to some brambles, skulked about, and then went into cover among the undergrowth. Sinéad headed for the cliffs. Lapwings flew overhead. She watched as the large flock tumbled from the sky and alighted in a nearby meadow.

When she reached the cliffs she sat on her favourite rock and gazed off across the soft green waters. A sharp kee-kee-kee-kee call startled her. She turned to see where the noise was coming from and just caught sight of a female merlin falcon darting across the bog being mobbed by two hooded crows. Then it seemed to vanish as her plumage blended with the colours of the bog. The crows flew away cawing loudly.

Sinéad sat for a long time lost in troubled thoughts. Who were the men at the cottage? Was her father in some kind of trouble? Why were those guns in the house? The very sight of them made her anxious. She forced herself to think of more pleasant things. She began to run through the whole enjoyable trip to Galway city in her mind like a film. A day like that made up for all the days of loneliness and isolation. She decided to return to the cottage and prepare Sunday dinner. Most of the villagers had gone to a fair in Clifden. She assumed her father would be gone too but as she neared the cottage she saw him talking with Peadar Walsh and Dingy O'Rourke. They were on Peadar's horse and cart. Sinéad knew it would be full of bottles of poitín for sale in the market. They set off down the road.

'Daddy . . .' Sinéad called after them.

Peadar pulled at the reins of the horse and her father turned and shouted back: 'I'm off to the fair in Clifden . . . do you want to come?'

'No thanks! I'll stay here.'

'Suit yourself,' he grumbled and they headed off down the road.

'Safe journey,' Sinéad called after them.

As they passed along the road they saw Danny approaching on a bike. He rang the bell loudly in greeting as he passed by the horse and cart. 'That's young Danny O'Sullivan, the Widow O'Halloran's nephew,' said Peadar.

'Dublin jackeen,' growled Billy Keogh, knowing full well where he was heading to.

'Ah he's a grand chap,' said Dingy O'Rourke. 'I was talking to him.'

'Hurry it up, Peadar, we want to get there early,' Billy barked.

'The early bird catches the worm,' laughed Peader.

*   *   *   *

Inside the cottage, Sinéad was rinsing out a shirt and some socks in a bucket when she heard the sound of a bicycle bell ringing and ringing. The bike screeched to a halt, then there was a rat-tat-tat-tat rhythmic knock on the half door.

'Salutations! Fair Lady! I come with a message, nay a decree from Her Royal Highness that you must attend a banquet in the royal palace, or to put it another way . . .' his accent changed to flat Dublin '. . . me aunt wants ye to come for Sunday lunch or else . . .'

Sinéad laughed, dried her hands and moved towards him.

'Where's the gilded coach and four white horses?' she asked in mock regal tones.

'Oh well, you see, the horses have the day off, being Sunday and all. So they sent me instead – a white knight on a black charger!'

As Sinéad looked at the bike, he tapped the crossbar. She laughed even louder. Then she hesitated.

'Maybe I'd better not, I have a mountain of work to do. I've to hang out those shirts, feed the fowl . . .'

'But, m'lady, you've been summoned. I shall lose my head if you refuse to come with me. Now you wouldn't like to see a poor white knight minus his noggin, would you?'

'I'll go, but first you must feed the geese and hens for me.'

'Your wish is my command.' He grabbed the wooden bucket with food scraps and some grain. 'Here chicky, chick chick, come and get your breakfast.' A goose pecked him in the leg. 'Ouch,' he yelled. 'You never told me it would be dangerous.'

Sinéad pegged the clothes to the line.

'I thought a knight was used to slaying dragons,' she teased.

'Slaying dragons is one thing, but greedy geese is another.'

'They're just excited,' said Sinéad.

'I know. It must be a big thrill for them to see me,' he retorted.

After Sinéad had finished her chores she got up on the crossbar of the bike and Danny gave out a loud holler as he pedalled furiously up the little rise in the road. Soon they were on a dip.

'Hold on tightly.'

Sinéad shrieked as they sped down the narrow windy road. Sheep on the road quickly jumped into the ditches. The brakes screeched to a halt when they reached the Widow O'Halloran's cottage.

The old woman came out to greet them. She indicated in whispered tones that they should sneak around the back of the cottage. Danny parked the bike against the wall and made big gestures as he moved around the back of the cottage. He pressed his body against the wall with his arms outstretched, then put his finger to his lips as he reached the edge of the side wall of the cottage. He swivelled his head, looking from side to side.

'All clear!' he whispered in mock fear. The widow looked heavenwards then pushed him on the shoulder. Sinéad laughed as he pretended to lose his balance.

When they reached the back of the cottage, there was Richard sitting on a stool, doing a watercolour painting of a rustic pole.

'Isn't it amazing how a rotten old post can be turned into something so marvellous,' said the widow.

'That's really good,' said Danny.

'Beautiful,' Sinéad remarked.

Richard smiled his thanks, cleaned the brushes in some water and they all went inside the cottage. They sat at the table and looked over the recent sketches and paintings Richard had done since he arrived in Ireland.

'Perhaps you will let me sketch you sometime?' he asked the widow.

'Me!' she said. 'Are you joking? Who would want to see a picture of me. Sinéad is a more fitting subject.'

'I would like to sketch the three of you sometime.'

'Fine with me,' said Danny. 'As long as you draw my good side,' he grinned.

'I hope you're all hungry,' said the widow.

'Starving,' said Danny.

'It's not very often I get a chance to invite people for lunch. Don't expect anything fancy like that restaurant in Galway.' She placed a large metal tray on the table. 'Shepherd's pie!' she said proudly.

'Mmmm, smells good,' said Danny. Then she placed a jug on the table. 'Lovely spring water from the well. As Sinéad knows I have the finest well in these parts.' Sinéad nodded. 'I have something a little stronger for us later,' she winked at Richard.

Sinéad really enjoyed herself, talking and listening to the interesting conversations. In her own cottage there were only grunts and growls from her father followed by long silences.

After lunch Richard made the widow sit for him while he did some charcoal drawings of her. Sinéad and Danny went for a walk. She felt so relaxed in his company; he was very interesting to listen to but above all he was fun to be around. He had such drive within him that it seemed he could conquer the world. They eventually made their way over to Sinéad's favourite spot on the cliffs. She explained how this was her secret place where she came most days.

'Tell me why you love it so much,' he coaxed.

'Here I feel so alive, so much part of the land, as the wind or the stones are.' He smiled at her. 'You think me foolish?'

'No,' he retorted. 'Not at all.' They stared off into the dark sea.

'It's a cold beauty . . .' she continued. Danny looked at her. 'It evokes feelings of awe and tenderness, yet it has hidden powers, it can be violent and unpredictable. Do you know what I'm saying?'

Danny nodded.

'Sometimes I think the sea is very lonely. At night I hear the murmur of the sea and I imagine it's calling my name.'

There was a sadness in his voice. She looked up at Danny and he placed his arms on her shoulders. She put her arms around his waist and they embraced. They stood for a long time just holding each other.

'There have been times,' she said sadly, 'That I felt I ought to give myself up to the sea.'

He held her at arms' length. 'What are you saying?'

'I really don't know.' She wiped away a tear. 'On winter nights I've watched the waves reach upwards to the sky as if to touch the stars. I could risk all, stake my very life on a whisper. The sea would release me from the bondage of this life of anxiety on the land.' There was a wild glare in her eyes. 'Sometimes I think the sea shapes my very being.'

'Well it certainly shapes your imagination,' he smiled broadly.

'You think I'm crazy, I know you do.' She seemed embarrassed at revealing her inner thoughts like that. She had never spoken like this to anyone before and now she felt vulnerable.

'Look!' Danny cried in excited tones. He pointed beyond the beach. Sinéad swung around. She could see the slow deliberate movement of the pod of dolphins out beyond the seashore.

'Quickly!' he grabbed her hand. They raced along the edge of the cliffs and headed down towards the sandy beach. 'I can still see them.' He raced faster.

Sinéad found it difficult to keep up with him. She almost slipped several times on the damp grass as they neared the beach. Danny leaped from a ledge and landed in the soft sand.

Sinéad pulled herself to a halt.

'Jump,' he said. 'I'll catch you.' It looked that bit too high. 'Jump!' he insisted.

She took a deep breath and leaped off the rocky ledge. She shrieked as she moved through the air. His strong arms grabbed her around the waist but her weight made him unbalance. The two of them crashed into the soft sand. They broke into uncontrollable laughter. Then he recovered, got to his feet and ran out onto the outcrop of rocks at the end of the beach.

The dolphins were nowhere to be seen.

'Ahh, they're gone! There were at least five of them.' Sinéad climbed on the rocks and moved out to join him. A rainbowing mist hung over the dark green sea. They sat patiently, watching and waiting, in the hope of seeing the dolphins again.

'What stories is the sea carrying?' he wondered in pensive tones. 'I'm beginning to sound like you,' he smiled.

She slipped her arm over his shoulder and around his neck. After a long time waiting they decided it was time to leave.

'They could be anywhere by now.' He gave a sigh of disappointment. 'Still it was great to see them, however briefly.'

'Look!' said Sinéad.

Danny turned and there they were jumping out of the water about thirty feet out to sea.

'Wow!' he exclaimed.

They gazed almost mesmerised by the movement of the wild creatures. Then one dolphin broke from the pod and moved nearer to the shore. It lifted its head out of the water and stared at the two young people. Sinéad and Danny could feel they were being watched; it was a strange sensation. It seemed as if the dolphin sought to bond with them.

Sinéad got the urge to leap into the water. She dropped her shawl, jumped in and swam over to the dolphin. The other dolphins appeared beside her. Danny threw off his jacket and shoes and dived in after her. They bobbed up and down in the water while the dolphins circled them and nudged them gently.

'Danny! Sinéad!' A voice could be heard.

They looked towards the beach and saw Richard standing on the shoreline. Sinéad waved at him. The dolphins slipped below the surface and disappeared out to sea. They saw them briefly about a hundred feet away porpoising towards the open sea, then all five seemed to melt with the waves.

Sinéad and Danny made their way back to the rocks. Richard climbed up to meet them and reached out his hand. Sinéad grabbed hold of it. He helped pull her out of the water, then extended his arm again for Danny pulling him up to the rocks where they had left their shawl and jacket. Sinéad lifted up her skirt and began to wring the water from it.

'That was a truly amazing sight,' declared Richard as he watched Danny squeeze the water from his woollen socks.

'Look at us,' said Danny grinning broadly. 'Soaked to the

skin. Look at my good suit.' He picked some seaweed from his trouser pocket. Sinéad burst out laughing.

'When I saw you go into the water after those dolphins I just had to follow,' he said to her. He picked up his jacket and a shore crab crawled out of the pocket. 'Aaah,' he yelled. This brought more hoots of laughter from Sinéad.

Richard smiled broadly.

'You two better get back to the cottage before you freeze to death.'

They headed back to the Widow O'Halloran's cottage. On arriving they looked in the window. The widow was still sound asleep on a chair facing the fire.

'That's the way I left her,' said Richard.

They lifted up the latch on the door and sneaked inside. Danny and Sinéad looked at each other and they both broke into uncontrollable laughter. The widow awoke with a start.

'What's happening? Where am I?' Then she became aware of her surroundings. Looking at Sinéad and Danny she declared, 'You're like two drowned cats. Is it raining that heavily? I better get the washing in.'

This made them laugh even more loudly and Richard couldn't help joining in. 'What ails you all?' said the widow. 'Go into my bedroom, child and put on something dry of mine,' she ordered Sinéad.

Danny went into the other room and changed into dry clothes. The widow made a pot of tea. Then she questioned them on how they had got so wet. Sinéad lay the clothes on the back of the chairs near the fire and placed a few more sods of turf on the fire. 'Well, I'm waiting . . .' the widow demanded.

'Young Sinéad here decided to jump into the water after a pod of dolphins that were frolicking about near the beach.

Before I knew it I found myself jumping in after her.' Danny gestured in mock innocence.

The widow's expression changed. 'I told you before, Sinéad, I'd prefer if you had nothing to do with those sea creatures.' There was an edge in her voice.

'They're quite harmless to people,' said Danny. 'In fact it is said that some seem to seek out humans for company.'

'They can be contented with their own company,' snapped the widow. Sinéad and the widow stared hard and long at each other, then the widow broke away. There was a long strained silence. She poured the tea and cut some bread and got cheese from the cupboard.

Sinéad eyed the widow again.

'How did my mother die?' she asked in a soft but determined voice. The widow became very tense but did not reply. Danny and Richard looked at each other.

'Listen, we'll go outside if you two need to talk alone,' said Danny.

'We're all friends, let's have no secrets,' said Sinéad.

The widow sipped her tea and gave a deep sigh. 'You're right, child. This country is full of secrets. Some of these secrets turn in on us and eat away at our community like a disease.'

The widow gazed towards the window as if she was looking out into another world. 'I had fitful dreams that night . . .' she began to recall the events. '. . . You know how your father and I don't exactly see eye to eye about things but the poor crathur was totally distraught the morning that your poor mother drowned although he tried not to show it. Your grandfather was nearly in a worse state. No one knows to this day how she drowned, her being such a fine swimmer. Of course the weather was shocking that morning . . .' Tears ran freely down her cheeks as she continued '. . . When we heard that those wild sea creatures had brought in her body we were all stunned.'

Danny and Richard looked at each other in amazement.

The widow wiped her eyes with her sleeve. She turned to Sinéad and looked at her lovingly.

'I suppose we should be grateful to those dolphins for bringing your mother's body back to us so that we could give her a decent Christian burial.' She reached out and clasped Sinéad's hands with hers. 'A miracle happened that day. You! For you were born that very day, you clung on to life, God bless you!' She smiled through her tears.

'We wrapped you in a sheepskin rug and we lay you beside a blazing fire to get the heat into you. You were like a little angel just lying there.'

Tears spilled from Sinéad's eyes. She opened her arms and reached out to the widow. They hugged each other warmly.

Chapter 13

The weeks passed. Autumn turned to Winter. Sinéad spent much time with her three friends and enoyed their company tremendously. She and Danny went for long walks on the cliffs, the wind buffeting their bodies or the rain drenching them to the skin. The sea showed its different moods, some days calm and green, at other times angry and foaming with crashing waves. The days ran into each other and Sinéad's habitual loneliness was, for a time, kept at bay.

Despite the bad weather Richard and Danny had set about restoring the old cottage. The new thatch had been put on it and, with a little advice from some of the old men, they had learned how to build and repair the dry-stone walls. They whitewashed the outside of the cottage during a break in the weather. Sinéad and the widow helped also, cutting brambles and clearing out nettles. Richard restored the old well and cleared all the mud and plants that were clogging the water's flow.

Once the cottage was fixed up on the outside with new window frames and glass, Sinéad offered to paint the windows and the doors. She had got a rose red colour paint from Johnny Mack. When she had finished they all agreed the house looked lovely.

The widow managed to convince them that her place with its new roof could do with a lick of paint, so Danny and Richard white-washed her cottage too and Sinéad painted her windows. The Widow O'Halloran was so pleased she decided to give Richard two of her prized oak chairs that had been given to her on her wedding day.

Richard was reluctant to accept them for he knew how much she loved them. Johnny Mack told him about a furniture sale that was taking place in Headford so Richard, Danny and Sinéad went to it. There he bought a wrought iron bed, a table, a wooden trunk, some stools and several other bits and pieces for the cottage, including curtains. Sinéad and Danny helped him arrange the furniture on their return.

When it was all finished the cottage looked very homely. Sinéad lit a turf fire and they made a pot of tea.

'Well, I have to say I'm very pleased with all the effort we've put into the cottage. Thank you both,' said Richard.

The Widow O'Halloran arrived with a large porter cake.

'Make some more tea,' she commanded. 'I've baked a cake.' They sat around and enjoyed the cake and tea. 'I hope you are very happy here, Richard,' said the widow. 'I'll miss your company in my place, but you'll have to drop in for dinner any evening you're passing.'

'Well everyone has been so kind to me since I've arrived here I don't know how to thank you all.'

'Have a house-warming,' suggested Danny.

'That's a very good idea,' said Richard. 'How about Saturday?' he wondered.

'Saturday would be grand,' said the widow. 'I'll pass the word.'

'Is that okay with you, Sinéad?' he asked.

'Oh yes, Saturday is fine.'

Danny sat looking pensive and sipping his tea.

'Everything all right with you, Danny?'

'Oh yes,' he retorted. 'Saturday is great. I'm looking forward to having a dance with Sinéad,' he grinned, winking at her. Then he added in serious tones. 'I will be leaving on Sunday.' Sinéad looked shocked. 'Well, I'd love to stay longer, but I've a lot of business to complete in Dublin. I meant to stay only a fortnight and I've been here nearly three months.'

'Oh God, we'll miss you sorely,' said the widow.

'I'll miss you all too.' After a long pause he looked at Sinéad. 'Would you like to go for a walk?' She nodded.

'See you two later,' said the widow.

The young couple walked silently for a long time passing the quiet fields. The moon hung low in the sky.

'The corncrakes are all gone back to Africa,' he remarked, trying to break the silence.

'They do make such a racket,' replied Sinéad, 'But you still miss the sound when they're gone. Do they really fly all the way to Africa?' she asked.

'Yes they do, and it is said they can return to the same meadow or field the following spring.'

'How amazing,' said Sinéad. Her arm reached out and she linked his. 'Wouldn't it be lovely to fly to the stars,' said Sinéad, 'or swim the seven seas.'

'You're a strange one, Sinéad Keogh.'

She stopped and stared at him. 'You think so?'

'I wouldn't want you any other way,' he smiled. They stopped and looked at the moon reflecting in a lake.

'I really am strange. You heard what happened to my mother.'

He put his arms around her and they held each other.

'We're all strange in our own way,' Danny said brightly. 'We'd find other cultures strange too.' Sinéad hugged him closer to her. 'It is very sad your mother drowned. But you're here alive and well.' He paused and said softly, 'The sweetest human being ever to come my way.' They gazed at each other. He slowly moved towards her and they kissed.

Suddenly there was the sound of horse's hoofs. A horse and cart came down the winding road. Two men could be seen on the cart, outlined by the silvery light of the moon. As the horse and cart got closer Sinéad pulled away from Danny, for it was her father with the stranger that had been in the cottage one night. The horse was pulled to a halt.

'Hello, young Sinéad,' said the stranger. Sinéad nodded.

Billy Keogh just looked at Sinéad and Danny.

'Do you want a lift home?' he grunted at her.

'No thanks, Daddy, I'll walk.'

'Good night, Mr Keogh,' said Danny.

Sinéad's father ignored him.

'Good night to you both,' said the stranger.

Sinéad threw a glance at the cart. There were several crates partially covered by straw. Billy Keogh tapped the horse with a hazel stick and it moved on. They stayed watching the horse and cart until it was gone out of sight.

'Your father doesn't say much,' said Danny.

'You'd want to live with him,' Sinéad retorted, then added, 'I wonder what's going on. I rarely see him these days. He's always making trips here and there. He never tells me where he's going or when he'll be back. I used to be sick with worry when he didn't return home. Now I expect him when I see him.'

'He's a sad man, all the same,' said Danny.

'Yes,' mused Sinéad. 'It must have been terrible losing my

mother like that. He must be very lonely, yet he won't ever talk about it. God knows I've tried to get him to, it might help him. It's not good to bottle up one's feelings all the time.'

'He will when he's ready,' said Danny.

'When?' sighed Sinéad. 'Will I have to wait another seventeen years?' Silence.

'It's getting cold these evenings,' said Danny, blowing on his hands. Sinéad stretched out her black shawl and draped half of it over his shoulders. The two of them walked to her cottage linking each other.

'Sorry I can't bring you in for a cup of tea, but Daddy is probably inside drinking his poitín with that man.'

'It's getting late. I better be going,' he smiled.

She cupped his face with her cold hands. 'It's going to be so lonely without you,' she said sadly. 'You've awakened beautiful feelings in me I never thought possible.'

'You're so very special,' he said, taking her hands in his and kissing them. 'I'll be back soon, I promise.'

Sinéad kissed him again on the cheek.

'Parting is such sweet sorrow,' he smiled, and walked down the road whistling *Molly Malone*. He jumped in the air clicking his heels. Sinéad stifled a laugh and watched him until he was out of view. Then she went inside.

Chapter 14

'God save all here!' Johnny Mack boomed as he entered the cottage carrying a crate of porter followed by his wife and daughter carrying several apple and rhubarb tarts.

'Welcome,' said Richard.

'Well you have the place looking lovely,' said Mary Mack.

'It's like a picture book cottage,' said Ciara.

'I hope that's a compliment,' smiled Richard.

'Oh, it is, it's gorgeous,' she replied.

'Well I had lots of help from Sinéad, the Widow O'Halloran and Danny there.'

Danny came over and greeted the Mack family.

'Hope everyone fits inside,' said the Widow O'Halloran coming over to join them. 'Sure, isn't it a dry evening? They can stay outside if there are too many.'

'Who would have thought the old McMahon place could look so good?' Johnny Mack remarked.

'Isn't it only grand to see new life and warmth being brought back to these old stones,' said the widow, touching the wall.

The priest arrived at the entrance of the cottage.

'Father Darcy, you are most welcome,' said Richard.

'Thank you Mister Anderson, for the invitation. I'll just make my way over to the fire. These cold evenings make my rheumatism act up something shocking.'

'Can I get you a drink?' Richard asked. 'There's some mulled wine if you would care to try.'

'Well, that would be grand; the last time I had that was at Christmas when I went to visit my relations in Kildare.'

'The blessing of God on all under this roof,' said a musician as he entered the house. Several other musicians followed behind him.

'You're going to have a full house, young man,' remarked a woman to Richard as more villagers poured into the cottage.

'The more the merrier,' retorted Richard.

Danny had been watching the door for Sinéad since the guests began to arrive but there was no sign of her.

'She'll be here,' said the Widow O'Halloran.

'I didn't know you were a mind-reader,' he teased.

'Now, it wouldn't be too difficult to read your mind. The pair of you have been like turtledoves since the moment you laid eyes on each other.'

'Ah here she is,' he said brightly. Sinéad entered carrying several bottles of poitín. Danny hurried over to her and gave her a kiss on the cheek. He took some of the bottles.

Sinéad smiled warmly at him.

'That's better,' she said. 'Those bottles nearly pulled the arms out of me. I was afraid I might drop them on the way.'

'Welcome, Sinéad,' said Richard placing his arm around her shoulder.

'Good evening, Richard. My father asked me to convey his regrets, but sent you six bottles of his home brew.'

'Well, that was very nice of him. Tell him thanks from me.'

Danny took Sinéad aside. 'Did he say anything about you being with me the other evening?'

'No, not really. When I went into the house he had gone to bed and the other man was sleeping on a couple of sacks on the floor. He was gone by early morning. At breakfast I finally decided to tell Daddy what the widow had told me about the day my mother died. He just burst into tears. I've never seen him cry before. He grabbed my hands and asked me to forgive him for being such a terrible tyrant of a father. I just sat frozen to the spot. "Can you forgive me?" he pleaded. He cried like a baby. I put my arms around him and I began to cry too. "You were a gift from the heavens but I was too stupid to realise it." It was the first time I saw the real man, the man who must have attracted my mother to him in the first place. Gone was the bitterness. I never knew anything else only his toughness and his anger. Suddenly it was all gone, all the poison. It was as if someone had lanced a boil and the pus was cleaned away.'

'Very descriptive.' Danny pulled a face.

'Sorry, but you know what I'm trying to say.'

'Of course I do!'

'I didn't want to leave him this evening, but he said he had to go to Galway; he was being collected by the men with the car.'

The musicians began to play several jigs and reels.

'My head is in a total spin,' she continued. 'I'm happy, sad, worried, confused.'

'What about me?' Danny replied. 'I came here to visit my dear old auntie and I'm suddenly on cloud nine and it's all because of you.' Sinéad blushed. 'Come on.' He dragged her into the centre of the room. 'Let's dance.'

The villagers looked on as Sinéad and Danny danced to the rhythm of the music. Soon others were out dancing on the floor.

'Isn't the energy of youth a grand thing,' said the Widow O'Halloran to Father Darcy.

'It is to be sure,' he replied. Then he turned to Richard. 'Perhaps you would like me to bless the house for you.' Then he paused. 'Oh, forgive me for assuming – but are you a Roman Catholic?'

'Well, I was brought up in the Anglican faith actually. But I'd be very grateful if you would perform a service in the cottage.'

The widow smiled. 'Sure Father Darcy, isn't there only one God after all.'

'Too true, Margaret,' he responded. 'What was it that the Dean of St Patrick's, Jonathan Swift, once said? There is enough religion in this country for us to hate one another, but not enough to make us love one another.'

'Well said!' The widow patted Father Darcy on the shoulder.

'Thank you for the mulled wine, Richard. 'I'm away now as I've a busy day tomorrow. Enjoy the rest of the evening.' He smiled at the people dancing and pounding the floor. 'You know, some of my colleagues would not approve of dancing,' he quipped. 'Sure isn't it grand to see people enjoying themselves. God knows life can be hard enough. Sorry I have to leave so soon.'

'Thank you for the candles and candlesticks, Father. Call in any time you're passing,' said Richard.

'I will to be sure. Well, I'll just slip away quietly. Matty Egan is giving me a lift back home. Good evening, Margaret.'

'Good evening, Father. God guide you safely home. Ah he's a grand old skin,' said the widow, watching the priest leave. 'Now if you don't mind, Richard, I'll open one of those bottles Sinéad brought. That poitín is very good for the chest and heart.'

'I'm sure it is,' laughed Richard as she watched her heading for the bottles.

Richard looked around at the villagers dancing and laughing, remembering parties back home that were always such formal, stuffy affairs. He smiled, thinking of what his father would say if he heard his son had thrown a party like this: 'Richard, you've gone native!'

'Well,' said the widow,' handing him a glass of poitín. 'Let's have a toast.'

'To what?' asked Richard.

'To the McMahon family who raised fine children in this cottage.'

'To the McMahon family!' They clinked glasses. Richard took a swig and began to cough loudly.

The widow laughed. 'That will clear your throat.'

'It will do more than that,' he remarked. 'It will burn my insides.'

'Ah sure it takes getting used to,' added the widow.

Johnny Mack came over to them. 'Fair play to you, Mr Anderson. A finer party I have not been to except the ones in my place.' He winked and grinned. 'Oh by the way, here's a letter for you, delivered yesterday to the shebeen.'

Richard took the letter. 'Thank you. It's from my father, I know the handwriting.' He put it on the mantelpiece.

'Come on,' said the widow. 'Let's have a dance.' She dragged him to the centre of the floor.

'Watch her, Richard,' said Danny as he swung Sinéad around making her shriek with laughter.

'I feel rather awkward,' said Richard. 'I've got two left feet.'

'Sure what matters as long as you're having a bit of fun.'

The party went on until the early hours of the morning. There was the sound of loud revelry as the villagers piled out of the cottage and headed home thanking Richard for a grand evening. Danny brought Sinéad home and said goodbye. He would be getting a lift early in the morning to Galway to catch the train. They embraced and he promised to write as soon as he got back to Dublin.

Sinéad watched him leave and waved sadly. She could see the pre-dawn light beginning to appear in the eastern sky. Wiping the tears from her eyes she sneaked over to her father's room and listened to see if he was asleep. There was no sound. She looked around. The fire had gone out and the cottage was in darkness. She opened his bedroom door but he was not there, nor had the bed been slept in.

Maybe he had gone with the men as he'd said he was going to. Sinéad was about to get undressed for bed when she noticed something from her bedroom window. Her eyes tried to make sense of the strange shape she was seeing outside. Suddenly she felt a terrible pain in her heart.

She slowly went out into the yard. There on the mountain ash behind the cottage hung the body of her father. He swung gently in the breeze silhouetted against the pale moon. She gave a loud scream into the night. The horse took fright and galloped off across the dark fields.

Sinéad fell to her knees on the damp grass, crying and sobbing. 'Why, Daddy, why?'

Chapter 15

A light rain began to fall as the funeral cortège wound its way along the narrow roads. The villagers were numbed with shock as they followed the two coffins from the church to the cemetery.

Sinéad stared at the pine coffins that the men carried on their shoulders finding it hard to believe her father was in one of them and his friend Dingy O'Rourke in the other. The Widow O'Halloran linked arms with Sinéad as they moved in silence. Mrs O'Rourke and her three daughters walked behind sobbing. Rooks lifted from their roosting elms and caw-cawed in the fading light as they circled the tops of the trees.

The wake took place in the O'Rourke's cottage with most of the villagers present. Sinéad thanked Father Darcy for allowing her father to be buried in consecrated ground.

'Well my child, it is a mortal sin to take one's own life, but I don't believe your poor father was in his right state of mind at the time. And as long as the bishop doesn't get wind of it, I don't think anyone will be any the wiser. I know the good Lord will look down kindly on their souls.'

Richard brought some tea over to Sinéad and placed his arm around her shoulder.

'Here, Sinéad, have a sip of this. It'll do you good.'

Mrs O'Rourke called for a bit of hush as she introduced a man from Galway city. The musicians stopped and the people looked at this small, wiry, red-headed man who stood up anxiously twisting his cap.

'Hello, I mean . . . good evening to you all. I'm Mickey O'Dwyer, a cousin of Dingy. I saw the whole thing, the way poor Dingy died. He died a hero for old Ireland.' There was a long silence.

Mrs O'Rourke nudged him gently. 'Go on Mickey, tell them how my poor husband died.'

Mickey swallowed hard. 'I believe Dingy and Billy Keogh were heading for Sligo. They were with three other men I'd never seen before. I was asked to meet them and to bring several boxes of ammunition. I had a pile of turf concealing the boxes in my cart . . .' he winked nervously for he could see the expression of the villagers had changed from sadness to shock.

'Well, I didn't hang around. I saw them load the boxes into the truck and head out the Galway–Sligo road. Apparently there was an army patrol waiting for them. I didn't see it myself mind you, but . . .' he hesitated, ' . . . there was a shoot-out. Billy and Dingy jumped from the lorry and made a run for it across the fields. The other three men held off the soldiers for ages, but they were shot dead. The lorry was searched and the rifles, guns and ammunition were discovered.

'Billy and Dingy got back to my place at nightfall. Poor Dingy looked terrible. He'd been pierced by a bullet. Billy didn't even know his friend had been shot until they reached my house. When Dingy finally agreed to let my wife look at the wound sure hadn't he lost so much blood that the whole side of his body was wet with it. He died around midnight. Billy must have gone home and . . . well.'

Mrs O'Rourke broke into heavy sobbing.

'Well, who would have believed it,' exclaimed Kevin Darcy. 'Billy and Dingy gun-runners.' There was a long silence.

Richard went over and whispered to the Widow O'Halloran. 'I'd better leave.'

She grabbed his sleeve. 'Stay!' she commanded. 'It's not the English people they're against, it's their government.'

Memories of the night Sinéad had seen her father with the stranger and the rifles on the kitchen table flashed across her mind.

'We're going home,' said the Widow O'Halloran. She hugged Mrs O'Rourke. 'God bless and keep safe the family and may poor Dingy rest in peace. Come on, Sinéad, you've had a terrible shock. You'll stay in my place tonight.'

They left silently, the widow and Sinéad linking Richard down the dark road. The Widow O'Halloran invited them back for a cup of tea. Sinéad sat in the widow's kitchen and tried to make sense of it all in her mind.

'Who would have thought your father and Dingy were into gun-running?' the widow remarked. 'They must have been very patriotic,' she added, wishing she hadn't made the comment especially at a time like this.

Sinéad sipped her tea. Richard sat staring at her. Slowly raising her eyes she said quietly, 'I don't think they were doing it for the noble cause of the freedom of Ireland. I think they were doing it for the money. Well, my Daddy was, I'm convinced.' They sat for a while saying nothing.

'Well wasn't it a lovely funeral,' the widow said brightly. 'The children sang like angels in the church. Father Darcy's words were so moving and what a big turn out.' No one said anything. 'Have some bread there, Richard,' she urged, after a time.

'No thanks, I'd better go.'

'Call over in the morning and join us for breakfast.'

'I will,' he smiled. He embraced the widow, then Sinéad. 'I'm so sorry about your father,' he said warmly.

114

'Thank you, Richard,' Sinéad said with a smile.

Richard pulled on a cap, wrapped a scarf around his neck and left.

Sinéad was grateful she didn't have to stay in her own house that night. She said goodnight to the widow and by the light of a candle she wrote a letter to Danny in Dublin telling him what had happened. She blew out the candle, got into the bed and lay quietly in the darkened room.

Tears streamed from her eyes.

Chapter 16

Sinéad had baked fresh bread and was making some scrambled eggs when the widow yawned her way from her bedroom. 'You're up early, child,' she remarked.

'I couldn't really sleep,' was the response.

'It's that oul' straw bed. I'm getting rid of it and getting another horse mattress for that room,' said the widow.

'Oh it wasn't the bed,' said Sinéad. 'Every time I drifted into sleep I could see my father hanging from the tree. It was horrible.'

'Hush, child, it's only natural you should be feeling like this. It was a terrible shock and it will take time to get over it. But remember time is the great healer.'

Richard arrived at the cottage and gently knocked on the door.

'Come in, Richard, and the blessing of God on you.'

'Thank you,' he replied, closing the door.

'You're up early too,' said the widow.

'Yes, I've been walking the beach.'

'Well I hope you have an appetite. Young Sinéad here has been preparing a gorgeous breakfast for us.'

Sinéad smiled. 'It's only scrambled eggs and potato cakes.'

'A feast fit for a king.' His eyes widened as the food was placed in front of him. 'How are you today, Sinéad?' he asked tenderly. He could see her red eyes with dark circles underneath, the eyes of one who had been crying through the night.

'I'm fine,' she said warmly.

'And what had you walking the beach at the crack of dawn?' the widow enquired.

Richard sipped his tea and took a deep sigh.

'There's something up, isn't there?' said Sinéad. 'What is it?' Her eyes were tearful as if she already knew what he was about to say.

'Well, I got a letter from my father the other day . . .'

'Is he all right?' the widow enquired.

'Oh he's fine. He works for the War Office; he wants me to go to the Western Front.'

'What?' she exclaimed. 'Go to war?'

'Yes. As a war illustrator.'

'Oh Richard,' cried Sinéad.

'Can they not send someone else?' said the widow. There was alarm in her voice.

'Most of the finest war artists and illustrators are already there. My father is afraid the war will be over before long, and I will have missed a great opportunity.'

'Sure you've been to war before . . . you said so yourself. I don't want to be saying anything against your father but I think you'd be better off here myself.'

Richard smiled. 'My father says I'm idling away here, restoring an old run-down cottage while most of the young men of the western world are out fighting the good fight for freedom and justice.'

'Don't go,' said Sinéad.

'Well I don't really want to go,' he sighed. 'I've really enjoyed my stay here and your wonderful company.'

'But you're going,' said Sinéad sadly.

'My younger brother is out there fighting, as is my sister's husband and they've only been married six months. Don't worry about me,' he said cheerfully. 'I'll be well protected away from the front-line action.'

'What about your lovely cottage?' said the widow. 'You have it looking grand.'

'Well I've been thinking about that. It was a lovely pipe dream but I know now I must go. Perhaps, Sinéad, you'd take it as a present from me?'

Sinéad looked amazed. 'No, I couldn't,' she said.

'Please, I'd like you to have it.' Then he grinned. 'Maybe someday Danny and yourself might get married and come and live in it.'

Sinéad smiled and looked embarrassed.

'Well, I don't know what to make of it all,' sighed the widow sadly. 'But if you must go, take good care of yourself. And come back to see us.'

The old woman walked into her bedroom and closed the door. They could hear her sobbing.

Richard stood up, gave Sinéad a kiss on the forehead. 'The cottage is yours, please accept it.'

Sinéad hugged him. She was lost for words.

'Goodbye, sweet Sinéad,' he said softly, then left.

Early next morning Richard set off for Galway on his bicycle, leaving a thank you letter to the widow and Sinéad, and several sketches he had made of the area.

*   *   *   *

Sinéad had another fitful night. She slipped out of the widow's cottage early and headed for Johnny Mack's with her letter for Danny.

'Good morning, young Sinéad. That was a grand send-off your poor father and Dingy got.' He crossed himself. 'May they rest in peace. Would you like to join me for breakfast?'

'No, thank you,' said Sinéad. 'I was wondering if you would be so kind as to get this letter delivered for me?' Sinéad produced the letter and some pennies. Johnny Mack took the letter.

'*Danny O'Sullivan.* Well that's a coincidence.' He pulled an amazed expression. Sinéad looked at him as he took a letter from a shelf. 'This one is for you, Sinéad.' Then he added, 'I couldn't help noticing the address on the back.'

'Thank you,' said Sinéad as she took the letter. Her hands trembled with excitement. She walked silently out of the shebeen and down the road. She opened the letter carefully and began to read as she walked along.

Salutations, my west of Ireland beauty.

On reading the sentence she smiled broadly and checked if anyone was looking at her. Danny wrote about how much he enjoyed his stay in County Galway and how Cupid had sent an arrow straight at his heart when he saw her. Sinéad paused, closed her eyes and imagined Danny speaking the words to her. She knew he had no idea yet that her father was dead. That sad news was on its way. She must write again this evening and tell him about Richard leaving to go and be a war artist.

As she read on then, her joyful mood changed to shock.

My dear Sinéad, I have taken the queen's shilling and signed on to fight for freedom against world tyranny. So many have signed up already. I saw a battalion of the Dublin Fusiliers leave the other day from the North Strand. They got such a wonderful send-off – it was very moving. A number of my friends signed up that very day. We will be shipped out next week, not to the front but to England where we will be trained to be soldiers. I don't know how long that will take, as we're just raw recruits. I hope we're trained before the war ends. Some people feel it might be over within six months. I will write again when I arrive in England. Take good care of yourself. Tell my aunt there's a letter winging its way to her by carrier pigeon (just kidding). Please give Richard my best, tell him I'll be fighting for his country while he's busy drawing little birds in ours.

I will write with my new address.

With love,

Danny

'What's happening?' Sinéad called out to the elements. 'Everything is going wrong.'

She ran and ran, clutching the letter, and didn't stop until she reached the sandy shore. Her heart throbbed and there was a knot in her stomach. She looked to the sky. It was grey and overcast. A light drizzle began to fall. She needed to swim to erase the pain she was feeling. The waters would soothe her, calm and relax her mental and physical pains.

She took off all her clothes and entered the water. It was bitterly cold as she had expected. Soon her body would get used to it, she thought, and after the shock of the cold she would be warmer than on land. She began to swim vigorously. Her teeth chattered, and goose-bumps appeared on her skin. She trembled, but forced herself deeper into the dark emerald waters, kicking and swimming. She was beginning to feel good and the tension seemed to leave her body with every wave that washed over her.

Then they came, looming out of the marbled waters. Their fins could be clearly seen as the pod of dolphins came closer in a steady porpoising motion. They made clicking sounds that seemed to probe Sinéad's very being. Even the water seemed to be energised by their presence. They circled her, brushing gently along her body as if to reassure her that there was no danger from them. She reached out and stroked their fins as they passed by.

Sinéad did not know what to make of their visit, but she enjoyed their company. The dolphins stayed for a short time, then they seemed to vanish like phantoms. She felt a sense of loss when they left. It was a very strange feeling indeed, like watching her family go away. Sinéad had counted five of them. They all looked similar but yet they were different, as different as people are to each other. When they came in search of her it was always a surprise, and when they departed there was a sense of loss as if they would never return.

Sinéad swam back to the shore and got out. The wind was rising and heavy raindrops began to fall. She dressed quickly and headed across the bog. When she got near her home she saw Ciara Mack up ahead.

'Ciara,' Sinéad called after her friend.

'How are you, Sinéad?' her friend enquired.

'As well as can be expected,' she replied. Then added, 'Would you like to come in for a cup of tea?'

'That would be lovely,' said Ciara. Sinéad busied herself making tea. 'The house will be very lonely without your Dad,' Ciara remarked as she sipped the tea.

'It will to be sure,' sighed Sinéad as she cut some bread and placed it on the kitchen table with some rhubarb jam. 'I miss him more than I thought possible.'

'And now Richard has gone away. He was nice, and a good artist. Not that I'd know much about art,' Ciara smiled. 'And Danny's gone back to Dublin . . .'

'The place is awfully quiet without them,' sighed Sinéad.

'I think that Danny O'Sullivan fancies you,' said Ciara with a twinkle in her eye. 'I've seen you two together and you like him too. Admit it,' she said.

'I do,' Sinéad smiled. 'He's wonderful . . . so full of life and he's got some great ideas for the future—' her voice began to quiver.

'What's up?' asked Ciara.

Sinéad began sobbing. 'He's gone to join the British Army.'

'You're not serious!'

'I am. He sent me a letter.'

'Why does he want to get involved with other people's troubles? Haven't we enough of our own right here in Ireland?'

'I agree,' said Sinéad, wiping tears away from her cheeks. 'He said it's a moral war and we've got to fight, otherwise the world will be taken over by tyrants.'

'I know a lot of young men have gone from these shores. Please God they'll be all right and return safely.'

'Please God,' said Sinéad.

'Well, would you like to hear a bit of good news?' Ciara smiled.

'Oh yes, that would make a pleasant change,' said Sinéad. 'What is it?'

'Sean Morrissy and myself are getting wed. We'll wait until I'm eighteen.'

'Sean Morrissy from Rosmuc?'

'The very one,' Ciara beamed. 'And in case you're wondering, my family and his approve of the engagement.'

Sinéad reached over and hugged her. 'I'm so happy for you.'

'Thanks Sinéad. Maybe you'd like to be my bridesmaid?'

'I'd love that,' said Sinéad.

'That's if you're not getting hitched yourself by then.'

'I doubt that,' retorted Sinéad.

'Maybe that silly war will be over by then. We'll have to get the banns* read out at Mass and my father hasn't even spoken to Father Darcy. So don't breathe a word of this to anyone yet, you know what the villagers are like.'

'I won't. Cross my heart,' said Sinéad.

*Banns: a public announcement of an intended marriage.

Chapter 17

June 19th 1915

Dear Sinéad,

I'm over here in England these past six months still training to be a soldier. If they don't send us to the front soon, some reckon the war will be over before we get there. Which would be a pity because we all want to play our part for world freedom.

I hope all is well with you. Thank you for the sprig of bell heather, it was very kind of you. I've written to the widow who seems to be in poor health these days. She told me she got a letter from Richard from Ypres in Belgium. Glad to hear he's well and in good spirits. He'll probably make a book of his illustrations after the war. I hope he does and that it will be a bestseller. I'm sure every soldier would want a copy as a keepsake.

I believe he's with the 4th Battalion of the Royal Fusiliers, in the 3rd division. I can just imagine him sitting there on a bit of a tree stump sketching with his pencil or charcoal, with bullets whizzing about his head like flies, and himself totally oblivious to them. Wouldn't it be great if we met up? Chances are very slim of course. I'm joining the Royal Irish Regiment of the 16th Irish Division. We'll be fighting alongside the 36th Ulster Division. Isn't it odd that our country will be united on the battlefield and we can't solve our differences at home. Life is strange. Well I have to finish now.

All my love,

Danny

P.S. Do write soon and thank you for the postcard with the thatched cottage on the bog and the turf creels outside the front door. I let on to the lads I was born there. They believed me!

December 24th 1915

Dear Sinéad,

Well, I've finally been made a soldier and I'm here in what's called the Western Front. It's a lot different to what I'd imagined. Someone said there are over four hundred and sixty miles of trenches from France to Belgium. I feel sorry for the poor farmers and their families who have seen the destruction of their fields for these trenches. There is barbed wire everywhere. The weather is terrible, rain and flooding. But everyone is in good spirits. I've learned a lot of songs since I joined the army. I've made many friends. There is a great sense of comradeship, of soldiers looking after each other. The cook from Lancashire is very jolly and he made a Christmas pudding for us in a German helmet.

I hope you are well. Please God the war will be over shortly and I will get to see you soon.

All my love,

Danny

P.S. Still no sign of Richard!

A heavy-set soldier moved over to Danny and looked him up and down. 'Irish?' he asked. Danny nodded. 'You better believe in hell, Paddy, because you've just arrived in it.'

Danny smiled dryly, and began to seal the envelope.

'Writing a letter to your girlfriend, Paddy?'

'Yes.' Then he added, 'The name is Danny, by the way.'

'*Oh Danny boy . . .*' the soldier began to sing, then laugh, then cough.

'I'm Ernie, I'm from London – East London to be precise.' They shook hands. 'Listen Paddy, I mean Danny. I've been here now over a year and my advice to you is keep your head down so no sniper can get a clear shot at it. And don't try and be the hero. That way you'll live longer and return home safely to your young lady love.'

'Thanks for the advice,' said Danny.

The soldier smiled. 'Here, have a biscuit and some cocoa.'

'Cheers,' said Danny.

'Thank God for the Tommy cooker,' said Ernie as he made himself a cocoa. 'I use rainwater, because those bloody water cans have leftover petrol in them and it taints the water. The biscuits are soaked in condensed milk; it's the only way to eat them otherwise you'd break your teeth on them they're so bloomin' hard. What a way to spend Christmas, sitting in wet trenches. Can't even go for a leak without some sniper trying to blow your head off.

'Even our own chaps are as bad. Last week a young fella from Bristol, I think that's where he was from, slipped over the trench to answer a call of nature. It was after dark and he was in some blooming crater. On the way back one of our trigger-happy sentries plugged him. We found him next morning lying on his back six feet away from the trench. Sad, very sad.'

'Don't worry, I'll be careful,' said Danny as he began to write in a little red-covered book.

'Watch what you write,' said Ernie. 'They censor the letters.'

'It's OK. It's not a letter. This is a journal of my experiences from the time I left Dublin to the time I signed up.'

'Well don't forget to write about soldiers' food – bully beef, hard biscuits and tins of jam.' He pulled out a small earthenware rum jar. 'Here, Danny boy, I drink a toast to you and to absent friends. He gulped down the rum, then passed it to Danny. 'Aahh that's good, it'll put the heat back into these freezing bones.'

Danny took a sip, then added, 'Happy Christmas, Ernie. I don't think the teetotallers back home would approve of us soldiers drinking on the job.'

Ernie grinned. 'I wonder what those Germans are thinking, Danny boy?' Ernie mused.

'Probably the same as us,' said Danny. 'Isn't it daft all the same? Most of them are probably farmers, bakers or ordinary Joes just like us. I'm sure they don't want to be here any more than we do. They're missing their families as much as we are'

'We better not let the major hear us,' said Ernie. 'He might think we're going soft.'

'Listen, guys,' said another soldier. 'There's going to be a cease-fire over the Christmas.'

'Really? That's bloomin' fantastic,' said Ernie.

'Pass the word,' said the corporal.

Over the next two hours, the soldiers moved back to headquarters. The major greeted them and raised a toast to welcome the new recruits. Danny looked around at the men who had been there a long time. Their faces were haggard, their eyes bloodshot and sunken in their heads. Clothes torn and ragged. The chef made a special effort with a tasty horseflesh stew. Some French units came and joined them. They had wine in their water cans which they shared willingly.

Cigarettes were passed around by the major and extra rations of rum were handed out. More men poured into the HQ. There were big cheers as Hughie Hayes and Liam Conroy arrived in with crates of poitín. The major welcomed one man in particular and asked if he would recite something. The soldier looked around at the men, took a sip of rum, then recited a poem he had composed.

'I don't know much about poetry,' said Ernie, 'But he sure has a way with words.'

'Who is he?' asked Danny over the loud applause.

'Sassoon, yeah, that's the name, Siegfried Sassoon. A poet and I believe a brave soldier to boot.'

Then another poet was called upon. He was Irish; his name was Francis Ledwidge. From his penny copybook he too recited some beautiful poetry that brought tears to the soldiers' eyes. The poems spoke directly to their hearts.

That night the stars, billions of miles away, seemed to come closer, a watchful presence over their heads. It was as if the young men were somehow protected under the twinkling heavens.

Then across the still air in the velvet darkness they could hear voices. The German troops broke into song, and recognising the air instantly as *Silent Night,* Ernie joined in. The chorus was quickly taken up by all the soldiers and the war was forgotten on that cold clear night; both sides were at one.

Chapter 18

The war was soon raging again. New Year came and went but the battle showed no sign of abating, if anything it got bloodier. Soldiers said it would get worse before it got better. Days passed into weeks, weeks into months.

Danny had several duties. One was as a runner from the front trenches to HQ, or from trench to trench with messages. Another was 'mining'. This consisted of tunnelling under enemy lines and planting a bomb to blow up the enemy soldiers in their trenches. The Germans had the same idea so Danny and his followers had to listen for any odd sounds as they dug their own trenches. Ernie was their chief 'lookout'. He would drive a stick in the ground and hold the other end in his teeth. If the stick vibrated, he knew the Germans were digging nearby. Both sides worked by candlelight and it was very dangerous.

Later Danny worked in CCS, Casualty Clearing Station, as a stretcher-bearer, moving the wounded men who littered the fields after an offensive. Four men were needed to carry one wounded soldier. It was an anxious time being out in the fields. Snipers would show no mercy and could hit a target from four hundred yards. Bombs constantly exploded around them; soil, rock and debris rained down as they ran back and forth with stretchers. Some of the wounded screamed in pain, calling for their mothers. By nightfall the soldiers on stretcher-bearer duty would collapse with exhaustion.

One morning Danny received a coded letter from his father. He deciphered from the cryptic writing that Dublin was burning and that Pearse, Connolly and the rest of the Sinn Féin lads who had taken over the GPO in Dublin at Easter had been executed.

Danny lay back in the trench and gave a deep sigh.

'Anything wrong, Danny boy?' enquired Ernie. 'Not bad news, I hope?'

'What a way to begin a century,' sighed Danny. 'With a world war raging in Europe and dear old Dublin burning down, with men of vision being executed.'

'Don't go worrying yourself about those big issues. Haven't we enough to contend with in these muddy trenches.

'Look,' said Danny. 'It must be spring.' A skylark hovered and sang in the air over a black cloud that smudged the sky. A meadow pipit alighted on some barbed wire with a beakful of nesting material.

'They're the wise ones,' said Ernie. 'God help them trying to raise a family among this carnage. Well, the luck of the Irish is with you, Danny boy. You've survived mustard gas, snipers, flame throwers, bombs, diarrhoea, eye infection, pneumonia.'

'You haven't fared too badly yourself, Ernie, and you're here a lot longer than me.'

'Well I tell you Danny, I know there's a bullet out there with my name on it.'

'Don't say that,' Danny scolded.

'I've seen too many of my friends blown to kingdom come. One minute you're with them chatting, having a smoke, next minute there's bits of them lying about, head separated from the torso, arms gone, legs . . . or some poor blighter bleeding to death from his wounds and no one can get to him. We're constantly under the strain that one of us is going to be killed or maimed any day Then at night there's the terrible sound of men coughing.'

Danny put his arm around Ernie. 'Come on, pal. Don't go down on me now. Who was it who comforted me when I arrived, a total greenhorn sitting in the dark trenches like a frightened rabbit? We're all in this together. The English, Scots, Welsh, Irish, Canadian, French, Belgian, and God knows how many more.'

'Even the poor bloomin' army dogs are out there wearing gas masks.' Ernie chuckled as a grin settled on his face.

'That's the old Ernie now. Just relax and I'll make us a cup of tea.'

Chapter 19

Sinéad sat on an outcrop of rocks with her feet dangling in the surf. The sea seemed so calm and untroubled. Yet she'd seen it on many occasions run wild with rage towards the shore, and watched it crashing at the cliffs with all its fury. Sometimes she felt that the sea was lonely and was calling for her. She imagined that the lonely waves would come to greet her and wished to caress her. She felt a certain comfort being near the sea. It was as if the sea were her mother, there to comfort her, especially at times like this.

Why, oh why had there to be a war? Why must there be enemies? She had been sick with anxiety ever since Danny had gone to the Western Front. How she longed to see him again. She cherished so much the letters he sent. She would always smell them first, hoping for a trace of his scent. He never revealed in his letters much about what the conditions were really like in the war. She knew these armies massed against each other were intent on one thing – killing each other. It must be all mud and blood.

The waiting was so terrible she felt at times she was going mad with loneliness and anxiety. Even poor Widow O'Halloran had gone into decline since she had learned that Danny and Richard had gone to war. How many others felt like this? Sinéad wondered. Who is it who decides war over peace? Is life not hard enough without all this killing? Are they so sure that God is on their side? Her thoughts pierced her like arrows. She gave out a loud shriek. Sea birds rose in flocks towards the sky in a frenzy of wings, only to return immediately to the strand line.

Sinéad stood up, threw off her clothes and leaped into the water. She swam as fast as she could out to sea. It felt so cold yet the water seemed to wipe the fearful thoughts from her mind like chalk being erased from a blackboard with a duster. She wished she was one of those dolphins; they seemed so contented in their watery world. They were able to roam wherever they desired in the great seas. She stopped and lay on her back and allowed the currents to carry her wherever they chose. She closed her eyes and floated in the silent world. She felt at one with the sea.

Voices sounded in her head, 'I will come for you, this is your home, this is the place where the ancient ones came from, I will bring you comfort, I do not seek to destroy you but to make you part of me. As the wave is at one with the ocean so you will be at one with me.'

What was happening? A different voice now sounded in her head. She recognised it, it was her own. There was fear in this voice. 'Am I drowning? Am I being sucked down into the depths? Am I to be buried in this cold silent world? Is this the way it must end? I'm afraid, I do not have the courage to join you. Am I of the sea? A sea spirit?'

The water began to fill her nostrils, life seemed to be ebbing away. She felt so tired yet so relaxed. Suddenly she felt her body being lifted up above the surface. She coughed uncontrollably. Water rushed from her mouth and nostrils. Her hands reached out for support. She felt the slippery skin of the dolphins as they swam grouped tightly together beneath her. Their bodies were like a raft; she lay across them and they carried her safely to the shore. They moved their bodies out of the water as far as they could and gently rolled Sinéad onto the sandy shore. Quickly they retreated back into the water and sped out to sea.

Sinéad pulled herself up onto her knees, coughing more seawater from her lungs, her body trembling all over. She looked seawards; all was quiet. She wondered had she imagined the voices. She felt so very cold. Quickly she put on her clothes and hurried home. She was glad nobody had seen her. She stoked up the fire and heated up some soup for herself that she had made earlier. She sat huddled by the fire feeling so very confused.

Chapter 20

Danny was sitting in a reserve trench writing in his journal one day when there was a loud explosion nearby. Bits of falling debris landed on him.

'Those Jerrys mustn't like what you're writing,' Ernie smirked.

An orderly sergeant hurried towards them bellowing: 'Here, you lot, grab a couple of spades and follow me. Some soldiers on their way to the communication trenches have just been buried by that Howitzer bomb.'

Danny and Ernie grabbed their spades and ran along the network of tunnels.

Danny saw the collapsed trench and a mountain of clay. Rats scurried about in a frantic attempt to find a new hideout.

'It's bad enough putting up with bombs, snipers, barbed wire, grenades but having to tolerate damn rats as well . . .' a soldier growled.

'Shut it,' yelled the sergeant. 'And see if any of these poor blighters are still alive.' Danny and the others began to dig fast and furiously. They found several dead soldiers.

'Keep digging,' the sergeant ordered.

In the end there were three soldiers alive out of the ten who had been buried.

'Thank you sergeant,' an emerging soldier coughed and brushed clay from his body. 'I'm Major Scofield. I have an urgent message for your company officers.'

'Follow me sir,' the sergeant saluted.

Danny and Ernie helped the last soldier to his feet. Still intact, he grinned at Ernie.

'You're bloomin' lucky mate,' said Ernie.

The soldier looked at Danny then broke into loud laughter and patted him on the shoulder. He continued to laugh.

'The guy's gone bonkers,' Ernie grinned. 'Come on, you'll be all right after a wash and some food inside you.'

They supported the soldier, helping him to the communication trenches.

'Well, well, Danny O'Sullivan. I can't believe my eyes!' exclaimed the soldier.

'You know me?' Danny asked. Then he looked hard at the soldier, whose face was smeared with mud. 'Richard?' he asked tentatively.

'Yes!' came the reply.

Danny could not believe it and hugged Richard and swung him about. They laughed uncontrollably.

'You two sound like a pair of laughing hyenas,' Ernie chuckled.

'It's my dear friend the painter, Richard Anderson,' said Danny, patting him on the back.

'A painter!' retorted Ernie. 'If there were more of your kind around here there'd be less killing and mayhem.'

'Oh thanks for reminding me. I left my portfolio behind in the rubble.'

'Bloomin' 'eck, not more digging,' sighed Ernie. They returned to the site of the explosion and began to dig.

'A year's work, I don't want to lose it,' said Richard anxiously.

'Is this it?' asked Ernie, lifting up a leather satchel with his bayonet. 'Well done,' said Richard.

They went back to base and fixed Richard up with food and drink, then spent the rest of the day relating their different experiences on the Western Front. And in the evening under the light of the Lucas lamps, Richard showed his portfolio of drawings and paintings to the company.

'You've certainly captured the scenes and atmosphere,' remarked an officer.

'Well the only things you can't capture are the smells,' quipped a corporal. 'The rotten flesh and the gases.'

Richard nodded in agreement.

Danny sat close to Richard poring over the drawings. 'They're great!' he remarked.

'To be honest,' sighed Richard, 'I'd much prefer to be drawing a donkey looking over a dry-stone wall in Cleggan, or a stonechat on a gorse bush instead of all this madness.'

'They're an important record,' said Ernie. 'Let the folks at home know what's really going on.'

Richard looked at Danny and smiled broadly. 'I have something for you.'

'Really?' Danny wondered what it could be.

Richard produced a drawing of Sinéad. 'There you are.'

Danny's eyes widened with delight then filled with tears. 'Thanks a million. It's excellent. God, I hope she's all right,' sighed Danny.

'I was sorry to hear the Widow O'Halloran is unwell.'

'Yes, my mother wrote to me saying she hasn't been well for months. She wanted her to come and stay in Dublin but you know my aunt "If anything happens to me I want to die in my own home."'

'She's a great woman,' said Richard. 'I wish I had known her for longer.'

'Sure, when all this is over we can go back and have a hooley,' laughed Danny.

'I left the cottage to Sinéad,' said Richard, 'as a kind of wedding present to the two of you when you're older and wiser and want to get hitched.'

'Well, that's really decent of you,' smiled Danny. Then to Ernie, 'Did you hear that? He's trying to get me married off and me only in my prime.'

Ernie looked at the sketch of Sinéad. 'You could do a lot worse than this fine young lady.'

'Is this the face that launched a thousand ships?' said Richard as the portrait was passed around among the soldiers.

Chapter 21

'These pineapple grenades are the business,' Ernie remarked, picking up his green canvas bag of grenades.

'He should know,' quipped Danny to Richard. 'You'd want to have seen him when he lopped two grenades, one after the other into a German pillbox last month. Took out the German machine-gunners in one go. A brave boyo,' added Danny.

'It's them or us,' said Ernie. 'And don't be fooled by your friend's baby-face, Richard. He's a crack shot with a rifle.'

Danny laughed. 'Remember when I called a rifle a gun in front of the officer.'

Ernie started to chortle. 'He didn't half bark you out.' Then Ernie began to mimic the officer in question. '"Listen, Private O'Sullivan, never let me hear you refer to your Lee Enfield rifle as a gun. Understood?" You looked up at him like a startled rabbit from a hedge,' Ernie teased.

'And remember the night we were on wire-cutting duty and we had to light the Bangalore torpedo under the wire . . . the badger that came out of nowhere and we thought it was a sniper? Well, that badger gave me such a fright I nearly ended up in brown trousers.' Danny laughed.

Joking and teasing helped the soldiers to forget the horrors of war, even for a short while.

That evening the Allies had succeeded in giving a devastating blow to the enemy. The dead Germans lay motionless, their twisted bodies mowed down and shot through with bullets. No frontline battalion would ever give up ground voluntarily, they'd rather die – and they did. The Allies were on a high after breaking through the formidable German defence lines.

'If this keeps up,' said Ernie, 'we all should be home by next Christmas.'

'Please God,' said Danny.

As they wandered around the dugouts they were astonished at the German trenches. They were like palaces compared with the Allied ones; they had wooden bunk beds, electricity, book shelves, a telephone, a gramophone, a variety of tinned meat, beans, fruit, and rice. Some of them were even lined with steel sheets, in stark contrast to the sand banks or wooden planks of the Allies' dugouts.

Tomorrow the Allied Troops would be on the move and away from the trenches.

'Won't it be marvellous not to have to hear the orderly sergeant bellowing along the front lines, "Stand to! Stand down! Fix bayonets!"' said Ernie with a grin.

They would be spending their last night in the enemy's trenches. Dawn and dusk were normally the most dangerous times for the troops in the trenches. Tonight they sat around in relative safety and took advantage of the German food supplies for their supper. A few rats scurried about hoping for scraps.

'Get out of here,' yelled Ernie as he pitched stones at them. 'Rats, bloody rats!' he growled. 'Still, when they go into hiding you can bet your bottom dollar shell fire will soon follow. They seem to sense it.'

'You know, a pair of rats can produce about 1500 offspring,' said Richard.

'Thanks for that,' grinned Danny, as he ran a candle flame along the seams of his jacket to burn out the lice.

'If it's not rats, it's lice or nits, or else it's bluebottles laying eggs in a wound. Before you know it, the wound is full of maggots,' Ernie sighed.

'Don't forget the red spiders and the ticks,' said Danny.

'All trying to sap our health and strength,' complained Ernie.

Richard made cocoa on the spirit stove and handed it to Danny and Ernie.

'Cheers mate,' said Ernie.

Suddenly a shot rang out. Everyone in the trench ducked. A lone German sniper slithered along the ground and took careful aim. A second shot rang out. All the soldiers, alert now, aimed their rifles into the darkness. A third shot shattered the silence. Danny could see movement.

'Danny boy,' whispered Ernie, dropping his rifle.

Danny looked at his friend. To his horror he could see blood spilling from Ernie's mouth. 'No,' he yelled, as his friend slumped down spilling cocoa over his body. Danny hugged him. 'Don't worry, Ernie. I'll get the medics; you'll be all right,' he assured him.

'We've been good pals, haven't we, Danny boy? Good pals!'

'Yes,' Danny wept, cradling him.

'My name was on that bullet, no one else's . . .' his voice trailed off and he lay still. There was a long silence.

Another shot rang out; a soldier next to Richard gave out a loud wail.

Danny pulled out his bayonet.

'No Danny!' said Richard.

'I'll be fine,' he sobbed. He crawled out into the inky night. Richard took his rifle and held it at the ready. He waited, his whole body tense. The minutes passed slowly. Was young Danny all right? Richard looked down at poor Ernie, his fellow countryman, still as the stones, with a gaping hole in his skull. There was a muffled cry from the other soldier beside him.

Beads of sweat broke out on Richard's brow. He took aim at the darkness. Then he saw Danny emerge, his bayonet, now covered in blood, was held tightly in his right hand, tears streaming down his face.

Next morning Danny received a letter from Sinéad. There were several small sea shells enclosed and a photograph of her that she had taken in Galway city. He held the small shells in his hands as if they were diamonds, and kissed her photograph.

Chapter 22

Months had passed into years. The Americans had joined the conflict. They too had lost many troops in this war to free Europe. Danny and Richard felt like veterans, having survived so much.

The loss of his friend Ernie was a heavy blow to Danny. Yet the Englishman was just one of the millions of young men who had died since this cruel war began. Danny was so grateful for Richard's company. They helped each other get through the madness of the conflict.

While Richard recorded the soldiers both living and dead, the weapons they used, the destruction, all captured with pen and paper, Danny continued to keep a journal. He wrote weekly to Sinéad and to his family in Dublin. He looked forward so much to any correspondence from home.

They had got good news that the German army was retreating. There was less and less combat where they were. Rumours were spreading that the war was winding down. Danny hoped so although he had heard it many times before. Since he had joined the war nearly two years ago, the conflict had changed month by month. The weapons of destruction had become more sophisticated with better rifles and better machine guns. Planes and tanks had become a feature of the battlefield.

As they made their way towards a small town in northern Belgium the sky was clear. Strong winds had blown away the heavy black smoke that had hung like a spectre over the land.

'Listen,' said Richard, stopping Danny in his tracks. Danny and Richard looked to the sky. They could hear the honking sound of geese. Then they saw the elegant birds arrowing their way across the sky.

'Geese!' said Richard excitedly.

'Yes,' said Danny brightly. His thoughts returned to his home in Dublin where he used to watch the Brent geese feeding near Bull Island during the winter months. It was such a beautiful sight to see them winging their way through the early morning light. 'I wonder if they're heading for Ireland,' Danny grinned.

'Oh to have wings,' sighed Richard.

'I'd be happy with a hot meal,' said a soldier as he passed Richard.

Richard smiled in agreement. As they entered the Belgian town the troops met no resistance. The enemy had been gone for several days. The place was like a ghost town: buildings charred from fire, beautiful houses scarred by bombs, bullet holes and fire, mounds of rubble everywhere.

A dead horse lay on the road, and several ravens were pecking at it. They lifted off on hurried wings at the sight of the soldiers.

Townspeople began to emerge from the shells of houses, greeting the Allies with open arms and hugging them warmly. An old woman kissed Danny and handed him an apple.

'Thank you,' she nodded, then turned to greet another soldier.

Richard sat on a broken wall and looked at a lovely fourteenth-century church that was reduced to a ruin. The roof was gone, and the stained glass had all been blown out from the windows. As he scanned the rubble he noticed something sticking out of the debris. Moving slowly towards the object he saw to his amazement that it was an icon in a wooden frame. It seemed in very good condition, despite the state of everything else. Danny watched his friend among the rubble as he bit into the apple. Then a sudden wave of fear and premonition came over him.

'Don't touch it!' he yelled to Richard.

His friend waved back, indicating it was only a painting. He bent down to remove it carefully from the rubble. Suddenly there was a loud explosion. Everybody stood rigid.

'No,' Danny shrieked as he ran towards Richard. When the smoke cleared he looked down in horror at his friend lying lifeless, his drawings scattered about him.

He felt a firm hand on his shoulder. 'Sorry about your artist friend.' Danny looked at the sergeant in disbelief. 'A booby trap, son, one of the oldest tricks in the book.'

Danny nodded silently and scrambled over the rubble to collect Richard's sketches. That evening he parcelled them and sent them to Richard's family explaining how his friend had died.

The soldiers stayed in the town that night. Richard was buried in the old cemetery outside the town the following morning. The next few days brought heavy rain. Progress across Belgium was slow. Mud and rain were their constant enemy as they had no shelter in the open fields. They passed through town after town. All were war torn, but the people always welcomed them.

One morning as they neared an old farm, the sergeant asked Danny and two other soldiers to scout ahead. The three men circled the deserted farmhouse and, covering each other, they kept a constant lookout for any activity. They moved into the farmyard, where chickens and pigs were foraging about, but there was no sign of anyone. They checked for booby traps but there were none. Danny signalled to the sergeant, and the company advanced.

One of the soldiers entered the hay barn to check for the enemy. All was quiet. He came out into the open. All clear. The other soldier looked at Danny. 'We can have bacon and eggs for breakfast,' he grinned.

'Good idea,' said Danny.

A shot rang out. Danny saw the soldier who had just come out of the barn, collapse in a heap. A sniper hidden in the loft took aim again, this time hitting the soldier beside Danny. He went down, screaming and holding onto his leg.

Danny dived for cover behind a water trough. Then he saw the German's rifle barrel stick out of an opening in the loft. He took careful aim, hoping to get a good shot. More shots rang out. Then Danny could see the side of the sniper's body. He fired. The German soldier fell through the opening, crashing to the ground below.

Danny went over and checked the soldier who'd been shot in the leg but he was dead. So too was the other soldier who'd been checking out the barn. Then Danny heard moaning. It was the German soldier. Blood was coming from his mouth and he was muttering something in German. Danny knew he must be calling for help. Danny moved cautiously over to him,

147

rifle firmly clasped in his hands. The sniper's gun was several feet away. The German lay gasping for breath.

Danny could see bright red blood oozing from his chest. He bent down and opened the man's uniform. His chest was in a sorry state from the bullet and the fall. The rest of the company entered the farmyard cautiously. Danny turned to indicate to them that all was safe, by raising his rifle with one hand above his head. Suddenly he felt a terrible, piercing pain. He looked down to see a bayonet stuck deep into his stomach.

The German soldier let go his grip on the knife and fell back down dead. Danny fell in a heap over the dead body. Two soldiers rushed over to check on him. Danny moaned and groaned as the soldier pulled out the knife and placed a rag on the wound to stop the bleeding.

'Are you all right, Paddy?' asked the sergeant.

'The name's Danny,' he retorted, managing a grin. 'And I've felt better.'

The medics came and attended to his wound.

*   *   *   *

Danny lay in a bedroom in the old farmhouse writing a letter to Sinéad. He'd been ordered to rest but felt compelled to write.

14th November 1917

Dear Sinéad,

My love, I have some sad news to relate. Poor Richard was killed several days ago. He was buried in a beautiful cemetery in the Belgian countryside. I know he'd approve. I was foolish enough to get myself stabbed. The pain isn't too bad and I'm resting in a bed. It's the first real bed I've been in for over two years. I had to get wounded to get a decent one. I'm supposed to be sent back home tomorrow, my injury is too bad for any more combat duty, so maybe it's a mixed blessing.

He coughed and some blood came out of hs mouth. He continued to write, hand trembling.

I don't know what the future holds, my love. But if for some reason I don't make it, always remember I love you. And if God allows spirits to wander the world, I will be in the soft winds that caress you, the waves that wash over you and in the song of the birds that serenade you. I feel so very privileged to have known you. Maybe we are what some people call twin flames, that were destined to meet in this life and in the next. I hope so. I'd better sign off now, my love, as I feel so very tired.
All my love,
Danny

'Hey Paddy,' a soldier yelled up the stairs. 'I've brought you a little soup to keep your strength up. You must drink it. Orders from the sergeant,' he grinned.

When he arrived up to the bedroom he saw Danny lying there, the writing paper alongside him on the floor. The soldier gently rubbed him on the shoulder. 'All right, Paddy? I've some nice soup for you. Sorry it's not Irish stew. Oh dear,' sighed the soldier. 'Looks like poor old Paddy's gone, God rest him.'

Chapter 23

Sinéad let out a loud shriek and sat bolt upright in her bed. Perspiration ran down her face. She looked around the room. Her body was trembling from a terrifying dream, where her lovely Danny lay dead in a pool of blood. She saw a movement, a shadow passing by the window of her bedroom. It was the shape of a man. Her heart started pounding in her chest. There was a loud rattle on the cottage door.

'Who's there?' Sinéad cried out.

'It's only me, Sinéad, Johnny Mack!' Sinéad threw her shawl around herself and hurried to the door. Johnny Mack stood there holding his cap tightly with his hands.

'Sorry for calling at such an unearthly hour, but I was over with the Widow O'Halloran and she was asking for you. Now, child, I know you've been staying over with her most nights since she's been ill, but she's taken a turn for the worse and I don't think she's long for this world. Father Darcy is there at the moment giving her the last rites. I brought her a drop of brandy last night, thought it might perk her up.'

He paused.

Sinéad searched him with her eyes. 'What is it?' she asked.

'Well, I also brought her a letter from her sister in Dublin. She nearly died on the spot after hearing its contents.'

'What did it say?' Sinéad pleaded. Somehow she felt she knew the contents already.

'Well, I'm sure she'd rather tell you herself,' he said awkwardly.

Sinéad hurried inside and got dressed. Johnny Mack had a jaunting car at the end of the lane. They travelled at great speed to the widow's home. Sinéad sat silent for the journey, wiping the continuous stream of tears from her eyes.

Father Darcy stood at the doorway of the cottage talking to Ciara who had stayed over with the widow.

'There's nothing more can be done for her. It's in the hands of the Almighty now.' He placed his hand warmly on Sinéad's shoulder in a greeting fashion. 'God bless you, my child. Now hurry inside. She's been calling for you since first light.'

Johnny Mack brought Father Darcy home. Ciara made some tea while Sinéad entered the widow's bedroom. The old woman lay still, eyes closed, rosary beads wrapped around her hands.

Sinéad tenderly touched her hands. The widow stirred. The once strong woman now looked so frail and old as she lay there. Her breathing was shallow and wheezing.

'Dear Sinéad . . .' she said weakly. 'How is my dear child?'

'Fine,' Sinéad sobbed.

'Give the old widow a kiss.'

Sinéad leaned closer and placed a kiss on her cheek and forehead.

'Hand me that letter, child.'

Sinéad took the letter from the shelf. A lump stuck in her throat.

'Sinéad, dear . . .' said the widow, her trembling hands clutching the letter. 'I hate that you should have to know the contents of this letter . . .'

Sinéad cried softly and kissed the widow's hands. 'I know already.'

'You do?' said the widow.

'Yes, I've been having the same nightmare for weeks. But I'd like to read what it says, please . . .'

Ciara brought in the tea and stood silently beside the bed.

Sinéad's eyes read the dreadful words and looked at the widow. They both began to sob. Sinéad threw her arms around the old woman. 'My poor Danny and our gentle friend Richard . . . dead in the prime of their lives. It must be so very hard on your sister in Dublin . . . ,' she added. 'It's terrible, shocking to think she would have received one of those awful telegrams.'

They sat in silent misery for a long time, then a serenity seemed to come over the widow.

'Sinéad, Sinéad . . .'

'I'm still here,' she answered.

'Sinéad . . .' There was a rattle in the old woman's voice. 'Sinéad!'

'Yes, what is it?'

'My child, when the sea calls, you must answer her.'

'What? What do you mean?' Sinéad asked.

'There's a lovely fragrance of flowers, can you smell them?' the widow asked softly, as if in a trance.

Her body went into a spasm momentarily. She jerked upwards then fell back onto the pillow. Now she was still. Sinéad gently closed her eyelids. Ciara began to cry hard. The friends tried to comfort each other. Then Sinéad took out a scarf as the old woman's mouth had fallen open, and tied it around her head.

*   *   *   *

The Widow O'Halloran was laid to rest a couple of days later. There was a big funeral for the old woman. All the villagers had turned up and followed the funeral procession from the cottage to the cemetery. They would miss her dearly, none more than Sinéad who now felt she had lost all her loved ones. Father Darcy said the heart had gone out of the village with the loss of the Widow O'Halloran. Sinéad nodded in silent agreement as she looked over at the poor old priest who seemed so frail and weak himself as he stood stooped over the grave, hands trembling, reading the final prayers.

After the funeral, Sinéad took Ciara aside and handed her a letter.

'What's this?' her friend enquired.

'Ciara,' said Sinéad quietly. 'I was given a present of the old McMahon place by Richard Anderson . . . and as you know it's a fine place to live in and raise a family. So I want you to have it as a present.'

'Are you out of your mind?' retorted Ciara.

'Listen, Ciara, read the letter when you get home. I have it signed over to you and it's been witnessed. It's like a legal document.'

'But why? I couldn't accept such a generous gift,' Ciara insisted.

'Ciara, you have been a good friend to me and soon you will have a handsome husband. Please God, some day you will have children as well, and when it's time for you to have a house of your own you'll have this cottage.'

'I don't know what to say, Sinéad.'

'I have this strange feeling I will soon be making a journey. I don't know where, and even if I don't go sure I have a place of my own here,' she smiled.

Ciara hugged Sinéad. 'Come back to my dad's place,' she urged. 'He's invited everyone to supper.'

But Sinéad wanted to be alone and headed home instead. The wind was beginning to pick up. It blew coldly in from the sea. As she walked the quiet road Sinéad saw the figure of a man in the distance coming up the road. He had a staff in his hand. As he got closer she recognised him as Hugh Lynskey, and as he passed her by he greeted her, then he stopped and laid a firm hand on her shoulder.

He stared hard at her.

'You! I remember you, colleen. I met you here a few years ago. You're a strange one, you're different, I can tell.'

Sinéad pulled away. 'What do you mean?'

'You're a changeling; you can't fool me.'

Sinéad became very frightened by his words. She turned and ran as fast as her feet could carry her.

The visitor stood waving his staff. 'You can't fool Hugh Lynskey, you're a changeling,' he shouted after her.

Sinéad didn't stop running until she got back to the cottage. She hurried inside and locked the door behind her. Her heart was pounding in her chest. The scholar's words had invaded her brain. *You're a changeling* echoed over and over. She ran to the bedroom and took down the small mirror and stared at herself, wondering had she somehow changed into some strange creature. All was well apart from her red eyes from all the crying.

She began to calm down as she moved quietly around the house. She looked at the fireplace – the fire had gone out. It was a bad sign; the old women used to say never let the fire go out of the hearth for if you do the family is doomed to leave the home. I need not worry about that, she said to herself, I am the only one left of the family.

She sat silently watching the dusk creep in over the horizon. Darkness had come early that evening. The windows rattled from the pending storm. Sinéad made herself some scrambled egg and tried to eat it but she had no appetite.

She tried to recall all those lovely memories of Danny, the

widow, Richard and herself when they were so happy together. She sat in the silence rocking herself to and fro on the stool.

It's time for bed, she told herself and got ready. She lay in a sleepless state in her darkened room looking out of the window and listening to the wind whistling around the cottage.

Sinéad felt somehow very vulnerable as she lay in the darkness, with a feeling of expectation that something very strange was about to happen. Outside, fierce winds blew; the tides were exceptionally high. The sea came pounding up the beach, then surged across the land.

Sinéad thought she could hear her name being carried on the wind. She trembled. The dark sea waters moved over the land like some creeping spectre. Sinéad could not believe her eyes: in the moonlight she could see that the water was lapping against the bedroom window, splashing on the glass, then it began crashing against the walls with a tremendous force. Now it was coming in under the door of her bedroom. Her room was filling up with seawater.

She was terrified. She shrieked with fear, but still it entered. Then the force of the water outside smashed the window. The entire room was enveloped, water swirling backwards and forwards in the darkness.

Sinéad began to float from her bed that had become completely submerged. She now realised what was happening. The sea had come for her. She remembered the old woman's words, *When the Sea Calls, you must answer her*. She decided not to fight the sea but allowed her body to relax, imagining herself floating on the waves on a warm summer's day. She closed her eyes as her body was lifted from the cottage under the cloak of darkness and carried away over the land out to sea. This was the way it must be, this was her destiny.

In the early morning light beyond the cliffs, six dolphins frolicked about on the sun-burnished waters.

The Sea Trilogy

Saoirse the Grey Seal

Don Conroy

MENTOR

The Mermaid's Song

Don Conroy

MENTOR

When the Sea Calls

Don Conroy

MENTOR

Wildfile

Don Conroy